His Babe

Emilia Olsen

Contents

Chapter 1 - New Beginnings

A lesha

I never wanted to get married or have kids. I just never saw myself fitting into those glorified roles of wife or mother. When my father died, I was left with my mother who was so broken her only semblance of worth was measured in the boyfriends she'd swap on a biweekly basis. Seeing that made me never want my happiness to depend on another person.

I actually felt sorry for my mom. None of those men were good people and she was obviously unhappy, but she disregarded all my warnings of them. Since my dad's passing, I wasn't her favourite person and, in all honesty, she'd changed so much that she definitely wasn't mine. Last I'd heard she'd broken up with the last guy for an old flame, one I wasn't too fond of. Her focus was always limited to whatever man she had in her life, so I cut my losses a while ago.

I could never be that caught up in a man. I hated the idea of going to school and working my entire life just to end up 'settling down' somewhere behind a white picket fence, raising kids and catering to some guy. While most girls had these dreams since they could walk and say, 'I do', for me somewhere down the line I lost the desire to stick around waiting for someone to come save me and take me someplace better than where I was. I could only depend on myself, not my mom, not my dad and definitely not some wannabe knight in shining armor.

I couldn't have any distractions stop me from leaving that place behind. So, school became a priority, I avoided boys and the trouble they would potentially bring and worked my ass off to graduate valedictorian.

Leaving for college I had my best friend Danielle by my side, the one person who I loved and trusted more than anyone. We were the only family each other needed. Her parents sort of divorced her while they were divorcing each other so it was like she didn't even exist anymore. They threw money at her and supposed she'd figure it out for herself. After graduation we didn't wait for our caps to hit the ground before we were on a flight to New York.

I'd gotten into Parsons with a scholarship and Dani refused to part ways, especially if we'd both be studying design. For tuition her parents didn't put up a fight paying out her $950,000 inheritance early as long as she didn't "come crying for any more money". They didn't ask where she was going to school and didn't bat an eye when we left.

We'd found a really cheap, crappy apartment in a shitty neighborhood that would at least keep a roof over our heads while we worked and went to school. Dani wanted to use her money on a high-rise apartment in upscale Manhattan for us, but I had to convince her to save it in case she runs into any trouble down the line.

We were beyond proud of ourselves and each other when two years into college, we were headhunted by big name companies, Dani for interior design and me for fashion. After a year with her company, Dani was scouted by some bachelor to design his mansion. She took the offer and ended up impressing the guy so much he hired her as Head of Design for his businesses.

She had been working with him for a year now and could not stop gushing about him and his super private upper-class family who stayed away from the spotlight. Her admiration of those people seemed a little biased since she's been dating his brother Rafael for 7 months now.

I couldn't disagree with what I'd already seen though. Whenever I played 3rd wheel it was clear they really were perfect for each other. He treated Dani like she meant the world to him and that was good enough for me. I was happy she'd managed not to let her past affect her the way I was unintentionally letting mine affect me.

-

All that led here, to me waiting for a blind date who was already 10 minutes late. Dani was obsessed with me getting away from work and actually living a life. Being 24 years old and harboring slight shame of my inexperience with the opposite sex convinced me to let her guide the reins of my love life.

I'm now regretting that decision.

Knowing Dani and the type of people she's been hanging out with, my date will probably be some trust fund baby and by the looks of this restaurant he picked, this guy probably oozes frat boy hoping to take over daddy's company. I overheard the host telling a couple that no walk-ins were allowed; at this point I'd gladly give them this table and go find a Chipotle joint.

I started chuckling thinking of what mindset I must've been in to allow Dani this kind of power. Looking up to find a waiter, I noticed a tall, bearded, dark haired man approaching me. Taking in his suave appearance

I try to prepare myself to not stutter knowing he probably just wants to borrow a chair for his wife who's no doubt a VS model.

The closer he gets the faster my heart starts thumping out of my chest and try as I might, I can't remove my eyes from his face because he is just that damn fine. Flicking the hem of his jacket out of the way, he dipped his hand in his pocket revealing how nicely the white dress shirt clung to his torso. Goosebumps. Stopping in front of me I see a cocky smirk resting on his lips. Not breaking eye contact, I return a shy smile embarrassed he's just caught me mentally undressing him.

"You must be Alesha. I hope you haven't been waiting long." He took his time examining my sitting figure, his eyes faintly darkening from a glossy emerald to a deep forest green. As my cheeks started heating up under his gaze, he realized my nervousness and continued with a smile. "I'm sorry for staring. It's just... Dani didn't really brace me for who I'd be meeting. Now I'm just a little pissed it took her this long. I'm Christian by the way." He pulled his hand from his pocket and stretched it out to me.

His warm palm enveloped mine sending a tiny shock to my nerves. He stood there looking down into my eyes as if trying to read my mind, not knowing the longer I held his hand the harder it felt to breathe. "Y-You're not what I expected either, but it's a pleasant surprise... Hi."

His smile widened to a toothy grin making his insoluble demeanor seem friendlier. Leaning down he pressed a kiss to the back of my hand before releasing it and taking a seat turning his attention to the drinks menu, I took in a soft breath, already missing his touch.

"See anything you like?"

JJ x

Chapter 2 - Wrong Assumptions

C hristian

I was definitely not looking for anything serious or otherwise, but Dani was determined to make me take her friend out. Every time she mentioned how supposedly perfect this girl was I couldn't help but roll my eyes. Having met a majority of the girls she hangs out with I knew I would only be disappointed; at least it'll end in a few fucks if she's hot enough.

The girls in our circle are spoilt princesses with high hopes they can live off of their fathers then eventually their rich husbands. They didn't feel the need to be educated anywhere past knowing how to give semi-decent head, spread their legs for any guy with a big enough bank account and hope to God they trap the poor man with a baby. Of course I want to be a dad but it'll be a cold fucking day in hell before any one of them was the mother of my children.

Yeah, I had a privileged upbringing of private schools, town cars and galas but knowing what my family did for a living always reminded me that we weren't like the basic 1%. I was taught that with our family holding such a respected role in our business, it was expected that each member maintain that reverence in whatever we did, especially when choosing who we bring into the fold. I could never raise my successor with one of these barbie wannabes, even though they were all that surrounded me. The closest I got to tying the knot was Charlotte, a mistake that almost found me making the worst decision of my life: settling.

My life as a crime boss was inevitable, but I didn't want my affiliation with the mafia to limit me. After my grandfather retired and I became Capo, I branched out and built an empire. Gramps had always stuck to mafia business not concerning himself with legal enterprises, but I needed to ensure that the Marino name was known in business, crime and law. With all my focus on work, it got easier for me to stop trying to find whatever type of girl it is I was looking for.

Dani's the first girl our grandparents had approved of so when she said yes to going out with Raf, I'm pretty sure my Grams was happier than him, now there was another girl around to soften the "overwhelming testosterone". For me it just meant that Sunday dinners were going to be a little less unbearable with my grandmother's pressures for grandchildren concentrated elsewhere. I trusted no-one except my family, so it took a while longer for me to warm to Dani outside of work, once I did it was clear to see why they loved her.

She's like the baby sister I never asked for, so it's pretty hard to say no to her. I figured I'd go on this 'date' to get Dani off my back and it wouldn't be the end of the world if I fucked another random priss. She told me to be on my best behavior because it's her best friend, somebody different from the girls we know but I was sure she'd be the same as the rest in the end.

*****

I'm a man that can admit when I'm wrong, and this is one of those times. I can honestly say I've never met anyone like her. She's smart, funny and sexy as fuck. It's been a few months since the date, and I can still remember everything that had me hanging on to her every word. I got to the restaurant a little early and headed for the bar hoping a few shots of whiskey could carry me through the night; and I figured if I saw her before I met her, I could leave if I wasn't interested.

I was a little taken aback when I heard the hostess ask for a reservation name and a soft voice replied with mine, looking up I was more than happy with what I saw. I watched as she sat down making herself comfortable, then I carried on observing in amusement as she scoped out the setting like it was the last place she wanted to be. It was charming how she seemed to be entertaining herself with her own thoughts. I figured it was time I stepped in, when she started chuckling to herself spontaneously; it was undoubtedly cute, but she looked uncomfortable enough to ditch, and I didn't want her to. As I walked over she took notice, the look on her face told me I would have her riding me regardless of how this date turned out, and I could not wait.

The minute I started talking to her, something felt off. It didn't feel like my usual bullshit chat where I ask them a couple questions and they answer with giggles. She seemed interested in what I was saying and I genuinely wanted to get to know her.. in every sense.

~

The girl is beautiful. She has this infectious laugh and a smile that pulled in blatant gazes from numerous guys throughout the night. Her unawareness of the constant ogling from men and jealous stares from their women entertained me, but trapped me in a space of wanting to hide her and show her off at the same time.

"My worst job?" She twisted her lips to a corner, looking to the ceiling in deep thought about the question. "When we moved here, I got a job as a waitress to pay my half of the bills, that was unquestionably my worst job. All the scumbags and creeps." She shivered at the memory and I couldn't help but smile.

"It's New York, anywhere you go you'll find scumbags and creeps." That made her laugh harder as she nodded in agreement. "Dani told me you're a designer now. How's that?"

"She's embellishing, I'm the mentee slash PA for the president of a fashion company, but I will say it's a lot easier to make the money when you love what you do." She smiled taking a sip of her wine. "...What else has Dani told you about me?" She asked, seemingly nervous to hear the answer.

Her hesitation was amusing. "Nothing too bad, just that you're the best person she knows and how you've managed to stick with one another through everything. Something I admire greatly; loyalty is important to us Italians."

She avoided my stare, bashful of the compliment. I started to wonder if she would be this shy with my tongue pressed against her clit while she tried squirming out of my hold. Picking up the bottle of red wine, I pour her another glass while she tuned back into my movements from across the table.

"So, what is it you do for a living?" She asked with a sincere interest in whatever my answer was to be. Her bright eyes bounced across my features taking me in almost as much as I was taking in everything about her.

Taking a second to debate flat out lying or avoiding the question altogether. I open my mouth to speak and find myself unnerved to say anything. I didn't want to lie to her, but I would never let someone outside the family know the truth. That wasn't an option.

"My family's business goes way back, it's extremely private though. I do own a few companies outside of that, just needed something to call my own." Omitting isn't technically a lie, is it?

"That's impressive, most people in your position would be happy with the security of a family name." She was right, a lot of the people I know are convinced their family's money will always be there, without even knowing where that money comes from. "You know I really wasn't expecting you. I was a kinda scared when Dani told me she wanted to set me up with someone from her New York crowd. All she knows are spoilt heirs and heiresses with money to burn- no offence." Catching herself, she covered her mouth fearing she'd upset me.

I laughed at how adorable she looked with eyes wide and mouth gaped. Those eyes ..that mouth ..those lips. I couldn't pull my eyes from the plump opening as I imagined how good it would feel to have them swallowing me whole.

"None taken. What kind of guy were you expecting?"

"I don't know, didn't really think about it.... gelled hair slicked to one side, khakis, boat shoes, 2 brightly colored polo shirts on top of one another and a sweater tied around your neck. You'd say something like "let's go to Vegas, I've got daddy's jet on standby".

I couldn't help but laugh at her assumption; the overblown uppity tone and partial truth of her imitation had me laughing my ass off.

"You just perfectly summed up half the guys I went to school with."

"Just half?!"

Her face had us both breaking out in laughter, drawing stares from other customers.

~

"Chris, did you hear me?"

I was pulled out of my thoughts by one of my soldiers Ethan. I've known him since high school, so he likes to think he's the closest thing I have to a best friend. He sat in a chair opposite my desk with a scotch in hand.

"I didn't catch that, what did you say?"

"I was telling you that Eduardo from the Mexican cartel offered us this months' shipment at half the price to avoid any potential disturbances from our men after what his cousin tried to pull last week."

"Tell Eduardo I'll take the next 3 months' shipments for free as his form of a generous apology. Also, let him know that the next time one of his men tries to stage a coup, I won't just kill the small army, I will wipe out their entire clan, so he better keep them in check."

"I'll make sure he knows. By the way Demetri called earlier and wanted you and Raf to know he's decided to extend his trip in Italy for another month."

"In that case notify the men we have over there to keep a close eye on him and let me know of any problems as soon as they come up."

"Consider it done." He took the last mouthful of his drink but didn't move to leave the room. "So... Danielle told me about the girl she set you up with, even showed me a picture. Cute. I thought your 'first date' was months ago?"

"No air quotes needed; it was a date. So what?"

"Nothing it's just Dani also said that you were with her Saturday night.."

"Ethan why the fuck are you keeping tabs on me?"

"I'm just surprised you've kept her around this long after fucking her. They're usually written off the morning after. You're either trying to stay on Danielle's good side or this chick is doling out some type of magic pussy" he started laughing expecting me to join in.

I usually didn't mind talking about the women I slept with, but there was an instant annoyance and irritation hearing Ethan compare her to the ones we've been involved with in the past. Alesha's nothing like them, she's the complete opposite, she's everything I used to wish they were when I was with them. I'd been hanging out with Alesha almost every day since we met, being with her solaced me.

"Watch your mouth. Plus, it's not like that. She's not like that. We haven't even- it's not like that, not yet."

"You haven't slept with her?! You really like this girl?"

I didn't reply and instead sat back in my chair taking a sip of the whiskey he'd poured for me. His eyes widened and his mouth dropped open in shock.

"Since when were you interested in someone for something other than sex? When do I get to meet her? Have you already run the checks? What about Charlotte? Does she know what we do for a livi-"

"I'm not an idiot, I ran her check when I ran Danielle's. She is definitely no Charlotte. Now stop with all the questions and go back to work."

Putting down the drink I turn my focus back to the paperwork in front of me while Ethan makes his way out of my office.

"And Ethan, refrain from talking about her pussy or any other part of her body. I'd hate to put a bullet in my so-called best friend, you know how I am, I'd have a hard time finding another one."

He left the room closing the door behind him. My mind drifted back to her with all of Ethan's questions running wild. He was right, I've never been interested in a girl outside of sex, even Charlotte was a means to an end. Alesha's different and I like it. All that played on my mind was how to make her mine.

JJ x

Chapter 3 - Model Behavior

- -

Alesha

It's been 4 months since Christian and I started whatever we were and having never been the object of someone's unwavering attention before, I can't deny.. it's flattering. I'm just a little confused because I don't exactly know what he wants from our situation-ship. He hasn't even kissed me yet. I've been trying to mentally dissect all these mixed signals and was getting nowhere. He would act super touchy and flirty whenever we met up, but by the end of the night that's all it was, flirting. He has to know I'm interested because I'm always flirting back. At least I think I am. This is the second-guessing part of relationships I've always dreaded.

We've already grown so close, learning almost everything there was to know about one another. I knew about his grandparents raising him and his brothers after his parents passed away and I didn't feel the usual reluctance explaining my relationship with my mother, or my father's death.

He went on to tell me about his companies in property sales and how in his business, people were always scared of him and he liked it that way.

Intimidated, sure, but I could never imagine someone being scared of the sweet, funny guy that I was spending most of my time with. Real estate must be a vicious game.

The more I learned about Christian, the more I found myself thinking about him, and wanting him. If it's a friendship he wanted, he wasn't making it easy. There was no denying my attraction to him and according to Dani we should "just spare everyone the back and forth and fuck already."

Lately, we've gotten into the habit of spending most the day talking about everything and anything from the minute we woke up. Today was not one of those days. I didn't get the usual 'good morning' text, so I sent him one instead, no reply. I'm gonna call him during my lunch break to check if he's alright, but until then I had a shit ton of work to do.

I'm done toeing the line, today I'll find out if he's interested in me or not. It's been months, I can't waste any more time wondering. I'm nervous and hope he says yes but if he doesn't, I still have the option of crawling into a hole and dying of embarrassment. 45 minutes until my lunch break and I'll get my answer.

My boss Richard tapped my shoulder trying to get my attention. "You look like you're having second thoughts? Don't. I love this layout, it's perfect for the Siriano dress, you did good kid." We were currently standing in the brightly lit studio while a photographer shouted directions to the model I had styled. This was my first solo project, designing and creating the cover of this week's issue of the company magazine. I was so proud seeing it all come together knowing I had prepared everything on my own.

"Thank you. The dress was the most eye catching of the collection and the floral detailing plays so well off the set it'll look amazing on the cover, but that's not what I'm worried about."

"That boy you're dating? I told you these New York trust fund babies aren't good for you. They're entitled and act above everyone else. I'm surprised someone as smart and skilled as you would even give one of those boys a chance. Not to mention, you're way too beautiful to ignore the eligible flock of men trying to pursue you."

I raise a brow and roll my eyes at the familiar words that Richard has told me so many times before. "I know. I warned myself about those reckless rich kids, but he isn't like that. He's actually really kind and charming and sweet.. and hot." I made my way over to the model to adjust the dress as he followed closely. "He's not what I expected so I'm gonna give him a chance until he proves me wrong."

Looking behind me, I chuckle when I catch him rolling his eyes and bring my attention back to the model making the necessary adjustments on the dress.

"Okay, just make sure he knows if he fucks up, I'll be the one he'll have to answer to. Does Mr Perfect have a name?"

"I don't know if you'll know of him, I didn't. His family is super private, try to stay away from "upper class drama". Christian Marino DeLuca."

The model must've been listening, she spun around to face me so fast, I pricked myself with the safety pin I was using to cinch the waist of the dress.

"OWW!"

"Christian DeLuca is the guy you've been seeing?" Richard asked shocked and wide eyed.

I gave a small nod before his face hazed over with an unreadable expression. Snapping out of it he gave my arm a rub and took the pin to finish the alterations.

"You're dating Christian?!" the model's voice rose slightly as she looked me up and down in disbelief.

"Something like that. Why? Do either of you know him?" I studied her with narrowed eyes as I sucked on my bleeding thumb.

"Apparently not." Her face went stiff as she turned her concentration back to the photographer almost as if dismissing me completely.

We were in Richard's office looking over all the photos from the shoot, choosing which ones to send to the editors. He sat back in his chair while I leaned in over his shoulder. I stared at the model's face thinking about our interaction and how disappointed, almost angry, she looked when she realized Christian was the guy.

I eased back and took a seat on the edge of his desk. "Thanks again for trusting me with this project. Are you happy with how it all turned out?" I questioned trying to brush away the vulnerability I felt.

"I told you I loved it. You did a great job. After working under me for so long, there's no-one that deserves it more." He pat my thigh sending me a proud smile.

I hated when people would praise me on my work- I mean I loved them recognizing how much heart and soul I put into everything, but compliments always had me feeling exposed which led to an overwhelming shyness. Skipping over all that awkwardness, I looked over to the large clock mounted on the wall noticing it was time for lunch. Standing from his desk, I slip my heels back on, getting ready to leave.

"If I don't go now I won't have any time for lunch and the last thing you need is me stressed out, hungry and irritated. I'll see you in an hour and a half." I say waving my hand, walking towards the door.

"Your lunch is an hour."

I turned to face him with folded arms and a raised brow.

He must be playing right now; this man knows how stressed I've been about this cover and now it's finally over I deserve a break. He dropped his head sighing.

"Fine. Take 2 and don't say I never do anything for you."

"Have I told you I love working for you? I'll bring you back that rabbit food you like so much."

"Please stop calling my salads rabbit food. Enjoy your lunch." I turn back around with a smile on my face continuing my exit.

Picking up my purse, I rushed to the elevator before Leona from sales notices me and tries to stop me for another one of those gossip sessions. I take out my phone ready to call Christian once I get out of the building. I scope out the office while waiting and start grinning to myself when I hear the *ding*, I stepped in hitting the button for the lobby.

As soon as the doors open for me to get off, I look up from my cell and there he is. His bodyguards Antoni and Sebastian planted behind him, all three stood somewhere over 6-foot looming over my mediocre 5'3. I was surprised to see him, this visit reminded me of just how sexy he is. They were all dressed in black from head to toe but somehow, he still managed to stand out.

"Hey! I was just coming up to see if you wanted to get lunch with me. Are you busy?"

"Not at all, I was headed out for some food and about to call you actually. Where did you want to go?"

I exit the elevator giving him a small hug and kiss on his cheek while waving to the men behind him, subsequently heading for the front doors, the 3 giants in tow.

"Ladies choice. I'm sorry you haven't heard from me today; I had a lot of stuff to think about. A lot of stuff involving you."

I stop and turn to see if his face would give away any sign of what he meant, but nothing. "What do you mean stuff involving me?"

The corner of his mouth turned up in a cute smirk, he looked to his fidgeting hands then back at me. "I'd prefer you were fed when we talked about this. I know how you get when you've not eaten."

I nodded my head and shrugged which made him smile harder. We left the building and he immediately took hold of my hand, pulling me to walk closer to him. The habitual gesture only made me more irritable, it brought up that unsure feeling I hated so much. I stopped walking and dropped his hand earning a confused look from him. Before I knew what was happening and could stop myself, the words spilled from my lips.

"I don't like feeling lost or questioning myself Chris. I like you, a lot. Do you want to be with me?" Losing my nerve toward the end I could hear the uncertainty and shyness smother my speech.

"Uhh..."

JJ x

Chapter 4 - Good Enough

Christian

Me having a thing for this girl will probably end badly but it's been 4 months and I feel like shit every time I'm not near her. We'd been out so many times, but I was still hesitant on pulling her into my life. I knew she wasn't like the other girls I usually toyed with, so I had to come correct.

Every time I saw her all I wanted to do was rip her clothes off and just fuck her. Just thinking about her begging me to go harder and deeper made me stiffen. This want wasn't a feeling I was used to, and it isn't one I'm sure I like. It's simple, if I was horny, I would find some chick to handle it, but with Alesha it was different; it couldn't be some random girl, it had to be her. I needed her in my life before and after, so I shouldn't risk fucking that up right?

I know she's getting annoyed with the mixed signals I'm sending, hell, so was I. It's hard keeping my hands off of her when we're together I can't move past flirting knowing the potential threats of being with her. If she found out about what it is my family does, I would be surprised if she didn't run as far and fast as her feet could take her. Would I even let her go once she was mine? I've always been a selfish man, bringing her into this life just to keep her would be the biggest example of that selfishness.

I've been up all night weighing the pros and cons of being with her, but the list was not working in my favor. Every scenario ended with her hurt someway, somehow. I wanted her, only her and there's no doubt in my mind that I would probably kill any guy she even tries dating. Everything was telling me not to go any further and to spare her the constant fear, worry and anxiety of being with me. The pinging notification cut short my internal debate, I checked my phone and saw she had sent me a text.

AM : Hey. If you're alive, where was my good morning text? If you're dead, where was my good morning text? I know you're probably nervous about that investors meeting this morning, but don't be, you'll do great. Talk later? Good Luck

She has me grinning like a fool at a text?! What the fuck is she doing to me? Cutting myself off from her is gonna be a lot harder than I thought, but it's the only way to keep her safe and away from any of this shit. Throwing the phone down on my bed, I lose the nerve to text her back knowing from here on out we'll be nothing to one another. I won't like seeing her with anyone else and I can't promise I won't act on my impulses if we're alone. Complete disconnect is what we need.

I got up, took a shower and got dressed. My 'investors meeting' with the head of the Bratva was to discuss a merger of our organizations. I got downstairs, seeing my main guards Antoni and Sebastian at the breakfast bar talking and eating from a lineup of food. I walked past them heading to the door, they immediately got up following closely behind. Getting in the car, we made our way to my grandfather's house.

Parking in front of the mansion, we got out and headed for the front door. Since my grandma berated me about not having any manners that one time I was running late, pulled up and had my grandpa jump in the car, I've made sure to always say hey to Grams, no matter what. She opened the door with a bright smile, dressed effortlessly in a floor length yellow dress. She pulled me into her and kissed my cheek, doing the same to the boys behind me. There wasn't even a good morning before she started offering us food suggesting we were looking too thin. I rolled my eyes at the guys making their way to the kitchen for yet another meal.

Dressed in a sleek suit as always, my grandfather, Vincenzo, walked out from his study and stood in front of Grams, gently sweeping her into his chest, leaving a kiss on her lips then pulling away with a grin. I'd always looked at my grandparents as the epitome of what a marriage should be, one I had hoped to emulate in the future. I smiled watching their embrace until he lingered on her wrapping his arms around her waist and burying his head in her neck. His muffled voice finding its way through her big hair.

"Winnie leave the poor men alone. They are grown, they know how to take care of themselves."

She rested her elbows on his shoulders while combing her fingers through his hair.

"Maybe if I had some grand-babies I wouldn't have to be so caught up in the welfare of grown men. Rafael and Danielle are still going strong, remind him that it's never too soon to start a family when you know you've found the one. I'm glad they found each other, she's such a sweetheart. I told you Christian, there are lots of girls out there waiting to be snatched up by my handsome grandsons. You just have to know which ones to pick and which ones to avoid."

She threw a judgmental side eye my way so I knew that was a dig at my poor choice of exes, especially Charlotte. I couldn't help but smirk at the shady comment.

"Trust me Grams I'm working on it. If it was up to me, you'd have a house full of noisy kids messing with your stuff already. I don't think Alesha's ready for that just yet though."

"Who's Alesha?" Gramps asked looking just as confused but nowhere near as interested as Grams.

I felt my face heat up and mentally cussed myself for mentioning her to them knowing I was gonna end it before it even started.

"Oh.. she's just a friend of Dani's who I was introduced to a while back. Nice girl. Beautiful and smart as hell; almost as funny as you Grams. She's good people.."

I didn't realize I had trailed off until my Gramps cleared his throat causing me to look up at the pair who were staring back at me in shock.

"You must really like this girl. You never even spoke about that budget-cut trophy wife like this. You should invite her to dinner tonight, I'd love to meet her. I'll behave, I promise. It'll just be the six of us. I'll make your favourite and I'll even add in beignets with rum chocolate dip for dessert."

"Winifred, we shouldn't make the boys feel this is a life they need to pull others into. It's bad enough being the head of a business like this, but to invite someone you care for into it is a great burden to bear. I was just lucky when I met you, you refused to know any better."

"He's right. Grams, I'm not bringing her into this mess, it's been playing on my mind since I met her. This is the first time I've not felt good enough. You know better than anyone why it's not really something I wanna put her in the middle of." She nodded her head understandingly with a saddened smile.

"I get it, but don't ever think you're not good enough... for anyone. The man I raised is kind and worthy of amazing things. To say you're not good enough is to say I did a lousy job and I know I didn't half ass that shit. " We all broke out laughing.

I felt bad. I knew all she wanted was for my brothers and I to have some piece of normalcy in our lives. She made sure to learn about the family business when her and Gramps got together, so she knew what the traditions were and what was to come. That doesn't mean she hid her hatred for the idea of me or my brothers taking over.

My brothers and I were raised by our grandparents. I was 10 and Raf 6 when our mom and dad were killed in a gang war. Raf barely remembers them whereas everything about them was ingrained in my memory. But for all intents and purposes, my grandparents are the only parents my brothers have known.

The day Gramps stepped down we had a get together celebrating my rise of rank. The night came to an end and everyone was leaving. I went looking for her and saw her in my room clutching the necklace she always wore. I smiled remembering how I'd gotten her the piece of jewellery as a teen and offered to upgrade it numerous times only to be refused and accused of "taking away the sentimentality of the chain". Her sobs filled the quiet space. It hurt seeing her like that and I spent the next hour convincing her I would be fine. Gramps made it 50 years and I was his under-boss for the last 8. I was ready.

Grandpa met my dad's mom a year after he became under-boss. She gave birth 2 years later, realized kids weren't for her and left. Grandpa didn't feel the need to look for her, his words were "what do I want with a woman willing to run away from her own child?" He met Grandma 5 years after and immediately knew she was the love of his life. They got married after 3 months dating and have been together ever since. 49 years and they were still crazy for one another. They've had their ups and downs, but in the end, they knew there wasn't anyone else for them except each other.

She treated my dad as if he was her own which made Gramps love her even more. They tried having more kids but stopped after her 6th miscarriage. She was desperate to give him another child and give my dad a sibling, but Gramps saw how depressed and detached she started becoming so told her his truth: that he loved her regardless and they were already parents to a boy who worshipped her. My Grandpa made sure everyone treated Grams like gold. She doesn't know it, but bodies were dropped if anyone so much as disrespected her or worse toyed with the idea of using her as a pawn.

"Grandpa we should leave now; the Russians are expecting us in 20 minutes. Toni! Seb! Time to go!" I looked back to the man wrapped around his wife, narrowing my gaze. "Are you sure this work isn't too tiring for you? These are your retirement years, you're an old man now." I joked.

"You wanted me as your consigliere for a reason. Besides, I like getting out of the house every now and then. Keep in mind that no matter how old I get, I can still kick your ass." He grinned giving Grams another peck before making his way to the car.

The guys appeared from the kitchen, both leaving a kiss on her cheek before exiting the house. I did the same and made my way to the jeep.

"Remember dinner tonight. Even if you don't bring her I'll still be making your favourite!" Her slight southern accent shouted behind me.

***

The meeting with the Russians didn't go as well as planned. They wanted more merchandise and an okay for their guys to push product in our territory, but they didn't know they weren't dealing with a fucking idiot. It ended with some strong words on both ends but at this point if they didn't bother us, we weren't gonna bother them. Fuckers.

We dropped Grandpa off at home and were heading to my office. Honestly, I couldn't give 2 shits about handling more bullshit today. Looking down at my phone I'm fixated on a cute picture of Alesha making a funny face. I hadn't spoken to her all day and I know that was the main reason for my shitty mood. I instructed Toni to take us to her office. It's time I sorted this.

We pulled up in front of the high rise building and walked in. I remember when I bought majority shares in this company, I still know nothing about the fashion industry but Grams loves being first with the free designer clothes and it's still making me a lot of money. I walked to the front desk where a pale, brunette woman sat speaking into a headset, a fake smile plastered on her face. I lean forward resting my hands on the glass table between us, waiting for her to finish the call. Noticing me, she hangs up giving us a more genuine grin.

"I'm here to see Alesha Moore, what floor is she on?"

"You'll just wanna walk back there to the elevators and head on up to the 65th floor. You're Christian DeLuca, aren't you? I must say, you're a lot more handsome in person."

She giggled scribbling something on a piece of paper. I just stared at her blankly already bored with whatever is about to happen. She slips the note across the counter to my hand.

"Call me some time, I feel like we'd have a lot of fun together."

I look at the paper then back to her and make my way to the elevators. I could hear her scoff and slap the glass crumbling the paper. The boys stood behind me sniggering while we waited for the elevator doors to open. When they did, I saw her sweet face staring back at me. I've come to learn that it's typical of her to look this beautiful without even trying. It still surprises me though. Every. Time. The leather pants gripped her thighs exactly how I wanted to, and her jacket had a belt tightly wrapped around her waist showing off her curves.

"Hey! I was just coming up to see if you wanted to get lunch with me. Are you busy?"

"Not at all, I was headed out for some food and about to call you actually. Where did you want to go?"

She stepped out giving me a hug and kissing my cheek. I take in a deep breath of her perfume trying to soothe my jittery nerves. I kill men for a living yet this 5'3 beauty is the one that has me anxious.

"Ladies choice. I'm sorry you haven't heard from me today; I had a lot of stuff to think about. A lot of stuff involving you."

"What do you mean stuff involving me?"

She looked so adorable with her brows furrowed in confusion and the bridge of her nose crinkled up, I couldn't help but smirk. I was definitely not telling her about my decision right now. I've been on the receiving end of her wrath when she hasn't eaten, and it wasn't pretty. None of my enemies could strike as much fear in me as she can when she's hungry. Hangry.

"I'd prefer you were fed when we talked about this. I know how you get when you've not eaten."

She nodded and shrugged her shoulders making me smile even harder. The boys and I followed her as we walked through the revolving doors.

Being next to her made me want to change my mind, I'm not used to feeling this weak, but for her I didn't mind. Naturally, being so close I had to touch her, I just needed to feel her against me. I took her hand pulling her closer, trying to latch onto her intoxicating scent and how silky her skin felt under my touch. Suddenly I felt cold and kind of annoyed as she dropped my hand and took a step away from me.

"I don't like feeling lost or questioning myself Chris. I like you, a lot. Do you want to be with me?"

Her words rattled me, she's never been this forward, it was so sexy. The shakiness and hesitation in her voice wasn't hidden from me.

"Uhh..."

Her bluntness was new so it took me a second to take in what she had just said. I examined her face while her eyes darted around nervously. I was feeling even more stupid about giving up the chance to be with her. I'll just have to keep the family business a secret and hope she doesn't ask too much about it, at least not until there's a ring or a baby. I'm done making the case against myself, we would be great together.

Stepping closer to her I gently pressed my lips against hers. She felt unreal and tasted amazing, like.. mangoes? Warm, plump and soft. Getting a little greedy, I dropped my hands to her waist forcefully pulling her into me as I ran my tongue across her bottom lip begging for entrance, which she gave me. I felt her hands clasp around my neck while I hungrily wrestled against her tongue with my own trying to claim as much of her as I could. I could feel myself starting to harden against her stomach and I didn't have any intentions on stopping.

She pulled away breathing heavily with hooded eyes, reaching down to touch her lips as if unsure of what just happened. I wouldn't mind showing her again.

"Me wanting to be with you was never a doubt. I'm not perfect and you're the last person I would ever want to disappoint. There are things about me that you can't know yet. I know it's not fair to bring you into my life without full disclosure, but know that if you say yes now there's no way I'm letting you go. It's all or nothing. You still wanna be with me?"

"... Yes." She let out in a whisper still caressing her lips. The grin on my face didn't come close to summing up what that yes meant to me. This woman is going to be the fucking death of me, and I gladly accept that.

"Good, my grandma wants to meet you. We're having dinner tonight. I'll pick you up at 7. I've gotta go put some things in order so I'll have to cancel lunch, but I will see you tonight."

She didn't say anything, just stood dazed slowly nodding. I pecked her lips once more and watched as she started blushing a shy smile then turned to walk in the opposite direction. I kept my eyes glued to her while I spoke to the boys standing behind me.

"Seb, keep an eye on her. Don't let her out of your sight and be discreet."

Sebastian followed in her direction while I headed back to the car with Antoni. I needed to put things into place so she wouldn't pop up on anyone's radar and if she did, those people understood she was off limits.

'Happy' seems like a gross understatement. She wanted to be mine and now she is.

JJ x

Chapter 5 - Get It. Got It. Good.

A lesha

I'm meeting his family tonight. I've never had a boyfriend but I'm pretty sure this is moving a lot faster than usual. I mean sure, we've been spending all our free time together, but that was as friends. He's easily become the closest person to me after Dani, and I trust him blindly, but I can't meet his family as his girlfriend. I thought I'd have some time to get used to me and him before introducing 'us' to anyone else. What if they don't like me. What if I'm not good enough?

So many important questions were popping into my head but all I can think about is that damn kiss. I've been smiling like a fool since lunch because I couldn't stop thinking about it. That shit had me tingling in parts I didn't know could tingle. I have a boyfriend now? Your girl has a man. A foine as hell, bearded, tight abbed, ass grabbing man at that too.

I'm just happy I'm finally home so I don't have to hear the constant speculations about why I was grinning like a Cheshire cat. Thanks to the lobby receptionist Stacey, there was already a rumor swirling around the office that it was because I'm sleeping my way to the top with one of the company's millionaire investors. If I wasn't too bent on keeping my job, hands woulda been thrown. She was not about to get me to act outta pocket in front of these folks. I know Christian made a more than decent living, he was always drenched in expensive clothes, but he would've told me if he was one of the investors of the company I work for.

I was sitting on the edge of my bed going over everything that happened today when my phone started ringing. Turning to the flashing screen, I feel excited and nervous all at once seeing his image pop up.

A- "Hey, I'm kinda busy. I only have an hour to try looking good enough to impress my man's family. What do you want?"

C- "You always look sexy and I for one am always impressed. I just wanted to tell my woman to dress fancy for tonight. I wanna take you somewhere after dinner."

A- "Babe, 'sexy' is not the first impression I wanna give your grandparents. I need to give them good church girl with the biscuits and sides vibes. Do you wanna come help me choose?"

C- "I would love nothing more than to have you be my own private model, but I have to get some things done before I come get you."

A- "...Are you sure we're ready for this? We literally only just started and what if they don't think I'm the right one for you? What if-"

C- "Stop. As far as being ready for this, I've been ready for you longer than you know. We didn't just start, we've been together since that first date, it's just taken me until today to do what already should've been done. When I asked if you wanted to be with me, the second you said yes, you were mine and I was yours, so regardless of who thinks what, until you say otherwise you are the right one for me. To be honest even if you say differently, I'm not letting you go. Get it."

A- "Got it."

C- "Good. I promise they'll love you. I'll be there in an hour to get you so be ready and dress however you want, it'll all be coming off by the end of the night anyway."

A- I let out a playful gasp. "Christian Marino dirty ass DeLuca. Boy you are so nasty."

C- "I prefer hearing you call me babe, wanna say it again once more for me?"

A- "Goodbye Christian."

C- "Doesn't matter, I'll have you screaming more than that in no time. An hour."

I hung up and took the phone from my ear looking at it wide eyed. This man had me blushing and he ain't even in the room. Since the kiss I've had the most overwhelming urge to feel more of him. I thought I wanted him before, that was a tame comparison to what I was feeling now.

My virginity was never sacred to me, I just wanted a decent guy who I trusted to be my first and here's the perfect one saying all the right things.

After taking forever to search for an outfit, I finally settle on something modest enough for Christian's family but sexy enough for him. Taking a cool shower, I try to soothe the nerves and hormones running wild. I also took no chances and shaved everything from neck down.

After moisturizing my skin, sorting my hair and doing the bare minimum with my makeup, I put on the outfit taking one last look at myself in the full-length mirror. Damn I look good. The weight I had put on these past few months went straight to my butt and hips; a little stayed on my stomach, but I wasn't mad at it.

I've never been a skinny girl, I've always had curves, cellulite, stretch marks the whole shebang. Seeing my mom hate or love herself depending on the guy she was with, I figured out for myself at a young age to own my body because ain't no way in hell I'm gonna let somebody else tell me how to be me. I got distracted for a minute checking if I could pull off an emergency twerking in this dress if needed. My little dance was cut short when I heard my buzzer ring.

Looking out my apartment window downstairs I see the top of Christian's head in front of my building's door. I also can't miss the luxe town car parked with the driver posted beside it.

Walking out my front door I grab my jacket and purse heading downstairs. I open the lobby door and standing close enough for me to smell the familiar cologne I love, is Christian with a rose in hand. I look at him from head to toe beaming at how handsome he looked.

He stood still not saying anything, eyes roaming all over my body taking in what I was wearing with his mouth agape. My smile slowly died down as he looked on still not saying anything which had me second guessing my picks for the night.

"You don't like it? I can go put something else on if you don't mind waiting, I had another dress laid out in case." Not getting an answer, I playfully pout "I told you to come over and help me. I've never had to dress for something like this before. Wait here, I'll go change into something else."

I turn to run back into the building, but he lightly grabs my arm halting my movements.

"No, you won't. You look amazing. ... Damn." He ran his hand through his hair, tousling the strands.

"Thank you. You clean up nice too." His eyes were still inspecting my body, fixating on my legs and chest. "Are we gonna stand here all night or what?"

Letting out a chuckle, I try walking past him to get to the car, but he stops me with a tight grip on my waist.

Lifting my chin, he takes no time in smashing his lips against mine. Pleasantly surprised by the action, I let out a light moan snaking my hand around his neck hoping to deepen the kiss. I feel his hand slide down past my waist squeezing my ass. I gasp at his rough touches yearning for more and he wastes no time slipping his tongue into my mouth. The minty aroma feeling cool against the heat of my taste buds.

In no time he had my back pressed up against the door and all I could feel was the pleasure of his tongue ravaging every inch of my mouth, his harsh rubs on my backside and his gradually hardening member pressed against my navel.I wanted more.

JJ x

Chapter 6 - I Got You

- -

Christian

"We're gonna be late if you don't stop."

Her words were coming out between slow deep breaths. I tried to listen and stop myself, but my hands were still massaging her ass which felt so full and perfect in my grip and my lips felt glued to her neck as I nipped at her vanilla scented skin trying to leave my mark. Seeing her in that dress did nothing to calm the blood rushing from my head to my dick. Pulling my tongue from her collar bone, I bite my lip resting my head where I had just eagerly bruised her.

"I'm not sorry. I knew you were gonna look good, I just wasn't expecting this." I knew she could feel the pressure of my erection pressed against her, just as I could feel how fast her heart was beating. Easing off of her and seeing how beautiful she looked made me remember she was mine, making me smile at the thought. I took the jacket she held in the crook of her arm, there's no way she's blocking my view tonight. "This is for you by the way" handing her the rose I had brought with me; I take the chance to appreciate her body one more time. Deep breaths.

I've never been this desperate for someone before, but she was more than worth my full attention. My past purely consisted of super skinny models and heiresses who did their best to maintain a slender look, so Alesha's body was new to me. She had curves and full breasts and ass, so much fucking ass. She blamed me for the weight she recently gained, something I've never been more thankful for. Her body made mine crave her touch.

"Thank you. You're getting that look in your eye again so let's get out of here before you attempt round 2." She starts walking ahead of me to the car, I take the opportunity to scope her out from the back. It's settled, I'm buying her that dress in every color. With what I do for a living, I've always avoided religion, but in this moment, watching this woman in front of me, I know someone up there put in work. 29 years to find her, if I told her how serious I was when I said I wasn't letting her go, she'd be freaking the fuck out.

"Hi, I'm Alesha." she held her hand out to my driver Roberto who's been with my family ever since I could remember. None of my exes had ever even looked in the old man's direction let alone introduced themselves.

We both looked at her surprised smiling. He took her small hand in his and spoke with his thick Italian accent. "Good evening ma'am, my name is Roberto. I will be your and Mr DeLuca's driver tonight."

Opening her door, his attention stayed on her as she started to speak again.

"Nice to meet you Roberto. The "ma'am" is not necessary, Alesha, Lee, A anything but ma'am." She laughed stepping into the car.

Roberto looked to me to approve what she said. I won't lie a part of me cringed at the thought of any man, friend or foe, getting too comfortable with a nickname. I'd rather Miss Moore now and Mrs Marino DeLuca in the future, but I reluctantly shrug an okay.

"Okay A." She smiled moving to the other side to make room for me. "I like this one."

"Me too." I slid in the seat next to her and Roberto shut the door walking to the drivers' side and starting the car.

"You've never told me to call you A or Lee. Why does he get to?"

"You hardly call me by my name anyway, it's always babe, bub, sweetheart or something else. I usually only tell friends to call me A. Is that what you want to be.. a friend?"

"If friends do what I want to do to you, then we can be best friends." She chuckled as I rest my hand on her thigh allowing her to wrap herself around my arm.

We were only 10 minutes into the ride to my grandparents' house and I could tell my baby was already freaking out about meeting my folks.

"Why are you so calm? Have you really done this so many times already?" She joked making me laugh.

"I've never introduced any of my.. companions to my family. Not intentionally anyway."

She looked at me with confusion written on her face. "Companions? Weren't you engaged to that Charlotte girl? Lot of exes bound to jump out of this closet huh. Do I wanna know what number I am?" She laughed it off, but I could tell it made her feel a little insecure about her own inexperience.

"Yes companions. Most of the girls I ran in the same circles with and others I knew through our parents' parties, galas and dinners. I never dated them, it was always purely physi-" I stopped myself before I could dig any deeper. "Charlotte was a mistake. One I learned from and managed to escape, but a mistake, nonetheless. I never actually introduced her; I think it's because deep down I knew my gang would never approve so it wouldn't have lasted anyway. We were having one of our usual family dinners and she turned up saying she wanted to surprise me. My grandma almost beat my ass when Charlotte told them we were engaged." Her brows raised at the revelation. "You are nothing like the rest, so don't psych yourself out."

Giving me a small smile, she nods turning her head away from me to look out the window.

"Hey.." I squeeze her thigh my hand's been resting on, calling her attention back to me. "You don't have to be nervous. I got you. If it gets awkward we'll throw the conversation to Raf and Dani." We were now in a full on laugh just thinking about how dysfunctional those two have been acting lately. She already looked so much more relaxed, I just stared in wonder. I sat back while she rested her head on my shoulder and for the first time it all felt right.

The rest of the ride was filled with mindless chatter and stupid dirty jokes. We even made a stop so she could buy a bottle of wine and flowers because she didn't want to turn up empty handed. I got the gist that she didn't want me to pay when after the fourth time I offered she covered my mouth.

Once we got to the house, I helped her out of the car and we made our way to the front door. I held her jacket and the gigantic bunch of flowers that were way bigger than they needed to be, while she carried the bottle of wine.

Ringing the doorbell, she looked me over straightening my tie. I was laughing at her nervousness when the door opened revealing my grandparents. Grams' smile grew into a wide grin when her eyes landed on Alesha. Pulling her into what looked like a suffocating hug, she kissed her cheek before stepping back. I probably looked just as stunned as she did when my grandpa did the same thing a few seconds after she was out of Grams' hold.

I have never seen the man so much as smile in the direction of anyone outside the family let alone hug and kiss them.

Grams was beaming and sent me a wink before turning her focus back to Alesha.

"We're so glad you could join us sweetheart! Christian's been a little tight lipped about you. Do you want kids soon?"

What. The. Fuck!

JJ x

Chapter 7 - Blended

A lesha

I was dumbstruck staring at the older couple, frozen still by the question. There was silence as the couple scanned me waiting for an answer. I could see Christian in my peripheral rubbing his temple and I could hear his whispered cusses of frustration. All of a sudden, they both burst into a boisterous laughter.

"I'm so sorry sweetie, we couldn't pass up the chance to see the looks on both your faces."

I breathed a sigh of relief and immediately start relaxing and laughing along with them. Once the shit my pants feeling left, I was cracking up at their little joke.

The only one not impressed was Christian, who had an angry frown and was still shaking his head at his grandparents.

I squeezed his forearm motioning for him to relax, feeling him loosen up under my touch, I chuckle as the older couple hug and kiss me again.

"Babe these are my grandparents Vincenzo and Winifred, guys this is Ale-sha."

Studying the pair, I noticed how young they looked. If it wasn't for their graying hair they could pass for early 40's. Vincenzo was very put together in his slacks and sweater with a button up and tie, while Winifred managed to exude a flawless elegance standing barefoot in a white dress that made her caramel skin glow. Wait.. his grandma's black?

Christian sniggered when he saw the minor shock on my face.

Winifred looked to Chris, a slight confusion masking her features. "After our conversation this morning I thought-" She cut herself short turning back to me. "Never mind. Hi sugar, you can call me Grams." What con-versation?

"And me, Gramps." Vincenzo chimed in.

"Noted. Christian talks so much about you two, it's high time I put a face to the names and stories. These are for you." I handed Gramps the packaged bottle of wine and gestured to the bouquet in Christian's outstretched hand.

Taking the large bunch, Grams brought them to her nose inhaling the scent of the blossomed flowers. "They're gorgeous. Thank you, pumpkin, you didn't have to. To think he's had the Charlotte's of the world showing up on my doorstep." She mumbled the last part but we all still heard, making me and Gramps chuckle.

"Okay Grams, when does Raf and Dani get here?" Christian asked eager to change the subject.

"Rafael had to cancel, something about vetting Dani's new client. Instead, I have a surprise coming a little later on, but I know you'll love it. Come, you're letting in the cold." Her soft southern accent was so melodic and soothing but still held a commanding tone.

Stepping into the foyer I glanced around the open space distracted by the immaculate design of it all. "Your home is gorgeous. I don't think I've ever seen anything like it."

Winnie walked up to me linking our arms together heading for what I assumed was the kitchen. "Thank you, it better be after 49 years of my blood, sweat and tears. Gosh, you're even more beautiful up close."

"Have you looked in the mirror? You two must have the fountain of youth hidden somewhere in this place." I said staring at her unblemished face in disbelief. All she did was laugh and pull me along. I wasn't kidding.

-

Dinner was going well. Our conversations flowed so easily talking about everything including how I grew up, to reminiscing on 90's TV shows. Every now and then Christian would give my thigh a reassuring squeeze paired with constant ogling, most of which I caught through the corner of my eye.

An hour into dinner we were onto dessert which looked amazing. One bite into the beignet and I was sure they were a new favorite of mine.

"Grams, before I forget, what's the surprise you mentioned earlier?" Christian probed.

"Well-" The doorbell rang, interrupting her. "Speak of the devil and he shall appear." She got up making her way to the front door with Vincenzo walking ahead of her protectively.

The door opened and there was some distant chatter and laughter, before Christian could get up and go check who just arrived, I needed answers.

"You didn't tell me your grandma was black!"

We broke into a laugh at my remark. Looking up when we heard footsteps heading back in our direction, the couple appeared in the dining room doorway, this time followed by a very good-looking young teen.

"So is my baby brother." Christian whispered in my ear as he stood to hug the young man.

"Pup what the hell are you doing back from Italy?! No-one told me you were getting back. I would've come get you from the airport." I heard a hint of concern in his voice.

"I don't need my big brother tracking my every move. Your daily calls were enough, besides, I can take care of myself. Anyway, I couldn't stay out there any longer, ma and pops had me missing them every time they got me on the phone. I had to get back, no matter how many hunnies were begging me to stay." His grandparents chuckled, staring on at him in awe. "You can let me go now Chris, I'm good."

Releasing his brother from the tight hold, Christian looked him over inspecting him closely as if he was trying to find any changes. "I know, I just feel like I haven't seen you in forever. By the way, I don't care how many big boy steps you take you will never not have your brothers looking out for you."

"The calls were to make sure you kept out of trouble. We missed you like hell pup. I think that should be the last of your travels until you're at least 21. Knowing how wild you can get kept us up some nights." Vincenzo grinned pulling his grandson in for another strong hug, kissing his head.

Just seeing how close they are I couldn't help but notice the contrast between this family and mine. I would never have this kind of love, support and closeness with my mother.

"Will you let the poor boy go so we can introduce him to our newest member." Winifred scolded her husband. "Alesha this is Demetri our youngest grandson. Pup, this is Alesha, Christian's..."

"Girlfriend" Christian announced proudly with a smile, keeping his eyes trained on me.

"Oh, thank God. I've never been so ready to give you a whoopin' if you said otherwise" Winnie sighed.

"I would've given you the switch" Vincenzo added making everyone chuckle.

I stood snickering as I stretched my arm out for a handshake, to which Demetri sweetly raised it to his lips for a kiss instead.

"Hi Alesha. I hope you haven't had to suffer too much through dinner with my folks. I'm happy that Christian's finally with someone who makes him happy instead of the usual succubi he finds. He's talked about you non-stop since your first dat-"

"You must be jet lagged. Why don't you go take a nap and we'll hang out tomorrow when you're feeling better and not talking so much." Christian held on to his brother's shoulders pushing him out of the dining room in the direction of the stairs.

"It was really nice meeting you Demetri!" I shouted with a grin.

"You too! You should come hang out with us tomorrow if you're around!" As his footsteps retreated, I continued my conversation with Winifred and Vincenzo.

"Guys we'd love to stick around but I promised this one a midnight outing, so we should head out." Christian said walking into the room with my jacket in hand.

"Okay we'll let you go. Sweetheart it was so great meeting you. Don't be a stranger, okay?" Winnie pulled me in for a warm hug and kissed my cheek.

"I won't. Thank you for dinner, it was delicious. If you keep making those beignets, you'll be praying to get rid of me." She shook her head laughing.

"Now I know to make more when you come back. Make sure you take care of one another."

Vincenzo enveloped me in a tight hug. Before he could break away, he whispered to me: "a man only shows his true self to those he loves, you've seen the real Christian." He pulled back keeping his hold on my shoulders. "Who people are and what they do are two separate things entirely, remember that. You're a good woman Alesha."

I smiled back not fully understanding what it is he really meant.

***

"I told you they were gonna love you." Christian seemed so smug as he rolled up the partition with the press of a button.

"They're amazing. Ugh.. being around them makes you want that kind of love, doesn't it?" I gazed out the window recalling how loved up the couple seemed. They had an air of authentic happiness. One that was so easily enviable.

"Yeah, they set the bar kinda high, it's a good thing I don't mind climbing."

"You cheeseball." We chuckled as he poked my side in an attempt to tickle me. "We both know what happened last time you tried that, don't play." He winced and our laughter got louder at the memory of me falling off the couch and accidentally kicking him in the dick.

"Alright truce." He took a breath to calm down, before rehashing the topic. "I'm being serious though." I was confused as to what he meant and he could tell by my furrowed brows. He ran his hands down his face. "Are you really gonna make me say it out loud?"

"You're gonna have to if you want me to be part of this conversation and know what you're talking about." I chuckled nervously, as an idea of what he was preparing to say formed in my head.

"A, I love you."

I think I stopped breathing. I had an inkling of what was to come but it felt completely unexpected the moment those words trailed from his lips. His eyes were trained on me in an unfaltering stare, making my chest heat up. "You don't mean that. You can't just imply you love someone after a day."

"What are you talking about? It hasn't been a day, not for you and definitely not for me. Since we've met, I've spent almost every day with you and when I wasn't, I spent it thinking about you. Seeing your smile and enduring your obsession with Stuart Barbell-"

"Stephen Amell*, don't come for him like that."

"Point is.. even though we weren't official doesn't mean it didn't mean anything. Besides I wasn't implying anything, I'm telling you I love you Alesha. If I'm honest I've known since you took me through that fucking IKEA maze." I could tell he was trying to break the tension, but I was still in a state of shock.

I narrowed my eyes concentrating on the greens of his iris, trying to detect any lies but found none. "I know I have feelings for you, and I know I want you, trust me I do, I'm just new to this. You know I've never been with anyone or had someone say things like that to me. I don't know if I can-"

"This doesn't mean you have to feel or say anything right now. I'm just letting you know where I'm at."

I nodded my head taking everything in, thinking about what was stopping me from saying it back. "Truthfully, that scares the shit out of me so I don't know if I can say it yet, but I want to try with you. Just.. don't lie to me or hurt me okay."

"I would never hurt you."

He looked and sounded so sincere when those words left him. The need for him was more than intense, it was like a hunger. I leaned over snaking my hand around his collar bone to the nape of his neck, pulling him to me eventually closing the space between our lips.

I felt as he grew desperate for more than the sensitive pecks I doled out. Gripping my thigh, he pulled my leg across his lap so I was straddling him. Only his pants and my underwear separating our primal need for each other.

I felt in control. Licking his bottom lip, he got the hint parting them for me. My chest rose and fell against him as I arched my back pressing into him. His lips trailed to my collar bone nipping at the skin. Grinding my wet core against his hardening member, I couldn't help but elicit a stifled moan. Breaking away from me, he whispered in a low growling tone, "Don't ever hold that shit in."

My heart was pounding so hard and erratic in my chest, I could've passed out. But it felt too good to stop moving against him. He let out a deep groan gripping my waist tighter.

"We should probably stop if you wanna show me the surprise you had planned." I spoke breathlessly between moans.

"Fuck the surprise." Pressing the intercom on the door handle he spoke to his driver, "Roberto turn the- ahh fuck- just go back to my place."

JJ x

Chapter 8 - Trust Me

WARNING: MATURE SCENEREAD AT YOUR OWN DIS-CRETION

DO NOT READ IN PUBLIC SPACES OR WITH OTHERS AROUND IF YOU DON'T WANT YOUR BUSINESS OUT THERE!!

Alesha felt so much confidence right now, she was unsure of what came over her. She just knew it was long overdue. She had always been comfortable with Christian saying dirty things and touching her body, but that was their flirting. This was different territory they were about to step into.

In the car Christian couldn't keep his hands off of her. Not even giving Roberto the chance to get out and open their door, he had her slung over his shoulder running up the stairs. His deep laugh and her vibrant shrieks and giggles were the only sounds echoing throughout the quiet mansion. When he got to the master bedroom, which was about the same size as her entire apartment, she pat his butt before he sat her down on the edge of the bed.

Gazing up at him, she nervously bit her bottom lip noticing how lustily he stared back at her. His usual emeralds were now so dark they appeared black. He removed his jacket before undoing his tie, unbuttoning his shirt and throwing them all to the floor. Staring in awe at his chiseled stomach, she could feel her heart trying to escape her chest it was beating so hard. Leaning down, he locked his lips to hers, satisfying both their needs to taste one another.

Breaking the kiss, she stood up stepping away from him. He was thrown by her sudden need to get away from him. "Do you not want to do this, because we don't have to."

She shook her head, heart still pounding and hands trembling. He stepped toward her, staring expectantly, waiting for her to explain what she was thinking. Almost as if she read his mind, her thoughts rambled off of her lips. "I feel kinda weird about having sex with you in a bed that you've had sex with other women in." She threw her hand to her forehead slightly embarrassed. "It's not a big deal, I'm just overthinking things."

Seeing how nervous she was made him want to be patient and prove to her how much more she meant to him in these few months than they ever did in those lingering years; but another part of him wanted to strip that innocence from her. He wanted to be the only one she felt truly safe around. He wanted her to feel just as confident taking what she wanted from him as he was about to feel taking what he needed from her.

He stood in front of her pulling her hand from her face as he spoke. "Since I bought the place this room's been off limits to everyone, even me. Dani's been trying out some designs but that's it, no one has been in this bed."

His calming tone tried to soothe her, but her chest continued the rapid rise and fall motion as his bulge pressed against her stomach causing fresh goosebumps to form all over her body. "Why?"

Bringing his lips just below her ear, he spoke softly. "I hoped there would be one woman I would do anything for, so I kept this for her. Just didn't expect to find you."

"It's nice, Dani did a good job." Her words were shaky as she tried to breathe through the tickling sensation she felt as his tongue glided over skin.

He pulled his head back wearing a smirk as he raised a brow in disbelief. "You wanna talk about Dani right now or do you want to kiss me? Cause I can take care of what's going on and come back in 20 minutes." He teased adjusting the protruding boner in his pants.

She chuckled taking his face between her hands and pulling him to her. He imprisoned her lips greedily, their tongues eager to feel one another. Clinging to her with an urgency, he never wanted to let go. His hands wandered past her waist, straight to her ass. Grabbing it, he squeezed and massaged with fierce dominant rubs as he pressed himself against her. The action made her breath hitch in her throat as she felt herself getting wetter and wetter.

Running a hand over her back he searched for that aggravating strip of metal. "There's no zipper." She announced taking a few steps back trying to steady her frame and ignore the vibrating tremors in her abdomen.

He watched her movements closely like a predator to its prey, licking his lips to savor the sample he'd just gotten of her. "Take it off."

The command was so abrasive and powerful it scared the living shit out of her. It was the sexiest she'd ever seen him, his voice so deep and barbarous. Her body's instantaneous excitement where Christian was concerned was a natural reaction. The longer he stared the more sensitive her clit felt rubbing against the fabric of her thong.

She slid the straps of the dress down past each shoulder, forcing the material over her chest freeing her full breasts to which Christian bit his bottom lip trying to control his intensifying desire for her. His hand rubbed the swelling erection through his slacks, giving some relief to its ache.

Pushing the dress further down over her hips and to the floor, then stepping out of it, she stood in front of him in nothing but her heels and thong.

The realization that this was the first man to see her naked suddenly flooded her mind. Her insecurities began running wild as she looked over to Christian to see his eyes exploring every inch of her flesh. Immediately her imagination spiraled with thoughts of him criticizing each blemish, stretch mark or trace of cellulite.

Reaching down, she picked up her dress using it to cover her exposed body. Christian released a breath he had no idea he was holding and took two long strides over to her. Ripping the material from her grasp he threw it over to his pile of clothes, gripping her waist, he forced his evident erection onto her.

"You don't get to hide what's mine."

He pulled her in, knotting their lips together, feeling an unbearable need for her. Sliding his hands down to her thighs, he picked her up, wrapping her legs around his waist. Walking back to the bed he placed her down, parting her legs to kneel and lower himself between them.

His hands caressed her body, one massaging her breasts and pinching her nipples while his other stopped at her hot core. Moving aside the dampened material, he grazed two fingers against her soaking slit making her gasp.

"Fuck. Baby, you're already wet for me."

His voice was so low it mirrored a growl. She could feel the growing erection poking her thigh through his slacks while he massaged her swollen clit. She bucked her hips upwards, inaudibly begging for more.

Christian licked and sucked her breasts, watching her face contort as he bit down a little harder on her nipples. He teasingly lowered his head leaving visible marks of his ownership over her body, finally resting his forehead below her navel so he could breathe in her sweet scent. Pulling off her heels and thong, he spread her wider.

Latching on to her clit, he began to suck mercilessly causing Alesha to cry out in pleasure arching her back, pushing herself further onto his face. Without hesitation he slid one digit in her entrance grunting at the tight fit. Alesha was in a haze of bliss as he pumped his finger in and out of her with his tongue relentlessly lapping at her sensitive bud. Christian felt his dick growing painfully harder with every lick of her. Her essence was like nothing he'd ever tasted before and it left him craving more.

She grabbed a handful of his hair feeling the intensity build inside her as she peaked her release, but that feat wasn't enough to get him to stop. He sped up feeling her walls clench around his rough finger.

Holding his arm firmly against her stomach, he forced a second finger further into her, past her calming orgasm. Feeling the warm taut fit, his teeth nipped her bud as his breath hitched. He pumped faster curving his fingers upward reaching for her spot, he could see she was trying to fight the second rushing buzz that threatened to take hold of her body.

Having him tweak and twist her sensitive pebbles while his mouth and fingers attacked her pussy, Alesha couldn't find any words to stop him and she really didn't want to. It wasn't until the second wave hit her that his fingers retreated and his lips pulled away leaving her limp and breathless. Kissing away the tenseness in her abdomen, he made his way up her body; coating her mouth with his in the hopes she would taste just how addictive she was.

Her hands played in his hair as they kissed, she needed to feel him. She needed him to feel just as good as he was making her feel. She reached lower yanking at his belt to undo the restrictive strap, unbuttoning his pants and pulling the zip as low as she could, she broke the kiss with a bite pulling on his bottom lip. Flipping him onto his back, she hauled off his pants and boxers; her mouth dropped open at the sight of his bulky member springing from the cloth, slapping against the skin just above his navel.

All the breath she could muster was trapped in her throat. She was convinced: virgin or not he was going to rip her in half. Her confidence began to waver as the fear crept in. Looking up at her it was easy to see she was worried to go any further. Christian spun them so he was back in control hovering over her; his lips lowered to her ear kissing her supple skin between whispers.

"You scared to take all of me?"

Not able to form any words while feeling his heavy dick sway across her hip, marking her stomach with pre-cum, she nodded her head.

"Do you trust me?"

Before she could answer, she felt him brush the head of his cock against her clit causing a shiver to race up her spine. He did it over and over again, mixing and lathering himself in their juices. Her eyes rolled back as she basked in the sensational feeling.

"Do. You. Trust. Me?"

"Yes, baby I trus- OH MY GOODDD!"

"FUCK! Ti senti cosÃ bene" he gritted lowly as his eyes snapped shut.(You feel so good)

His breathing got heavier with a little more than the swollen head of his dick stuffed into her. Alesha's eyes were sealed as she dug her nails into his tensed shoulders; the discomfort was cuss worthy.

Keeping his hips still, he kissed every part of her body his tongue could reach, allowing her time to get use to the tension between her legs.

"Baby look at me."

Her head dropped back onto the pillow as she opened her eyes to see his forest green gems looking back at her. Light gasps for air left her lips as she tried to regulate her breathing.

"It's all up to you when I move, okay?"

She closed her eyes again, waiting for the pain to subside.

"Alesha, look at me."

Hearing the tenderness in his voice, she opened her eyes once more to find the same gem-like orbs staring back at her.

"It's just me and you. Baby, I won't hurt you. Just trust me."

He gazed at her as if she was the only thing that mattered. Nuzzling into her neck he proudly kissed the glowing love bites he'd left behind.

"Okay, I'm ready."

Her voice came out in a quivering moan. Their gazes were locked onto one another as he pulled from her. Pushing his dick into her inch by agonizing inch, she winced. He pulled out and achingly forced himself back in until he saw her flinches of pain transform to writhings and moans of pure pleasure. He loved being the one to make her feel this way.

The way her body consumed him felt like unfiltered heaven. Her sweet cunt engulfed him as he pushed his dick deeper and deeper until she was taking all of him.

Knowing this was her first time, he wanted to take it easy, but each thrust made it more and more difficult to control the want to fuck her harder. Baring his teeth, his jaw clenched when she started pushing herself further onto him. She wanted more just as he did, he sped up pounding roughly into her. Since the first stroke feeling how wet and tight her pussy was, he's tried to keep the unyielding desire to cum at bay, he wasn't sure he would be able to suppress it for much longer. She felt too good.

Hearing her soft raspy moans and feeling her body writhe under him were things he'd only dreamt of and now she was here, fulfilling all those fantasies. He dropped his head in the crook of her collar, inhaling their scent as their flesh slapped against each other, her gripping him tighter with every stroke. His senses were on overload.

"This is mine. You. Are. Mine. Any man so much as touches you I'll kill them. Say it."

"I'm yours. Holy fuck! Christian I'm yours." The authority and possession in his voice made her beg for more. "Yes! Harder! Fuck me!" His groans became deafening as he slammed himself into her ruthlessly, hands fastened to her waist.

This felt like an out-of-body experience to Alesha. She'd never felt something so tormentingly wonderful. Every time she climaxed, he would just go harder and deeper hitting that fucking spot she quickly learned to love. She'd lost count of the amount of times she screamed at the top of her lungs because of what this incredible man was doing to her body.

The building pressure in the pit of his stomach felt unreal to Christian. The intensity was unlike anything he'd ever felt before. His throbbing cock demanded more of her; his grip tensed delivering violent thrusts to her tight pussy.

"Baby, you're gonna make me cum! Fuck!"

He raised his head still forcing himself in and out of her with savage strokes. His deep grunts and groans were the only sounds escaping. Seeing the pleasure in those golden-brown eyes and hearing the soft gasps for breath from her parted lips only made his dick twitch harder inside her.

He attacked her lips with an insatiable need. Slamming into her twice more, she came undone once more. Feeling her pussy clench around his throbbing member again, forced him to let out a gritty groan as he buried his seed deep inside her; the rush spreading from the base of his gut to his head and toes.

Dropping his head to the pillow beside hers, they both lay there reluctantly coming down from the natural high. The only sound being heavy and unsteady intakes of breath as their sweat coated bodies relaxed on one another. He lifted his head capturing her lips again, putting everything he had into the passionate exchange.

"I meant what I said. You're mine."

Still in a haze, she just closed her eyes waiting for her body to cool down. He unwillingly pulled out of her and got up heading to the bathroom. She instantly missed how whole she felt when he was inside her.

No time had passed before he was back in the room with a warm washcloth wiping her down. She smiled when she felt him lay pecks on her inner thighs and stomach but shivered when he teasingly grazed his teeth over her sensitive nipple before leaving another peck on her lips.

"I know I was too rough for your first time, I'm sorry I couldn't help myself."

"I loved it."

"You're not gonna like me too much when you wake up sore."

"I'm okay. I promise."

He headed back to the bathroom and she threw her arm over her eyes drifting off to sleep.

Walking back into the room he examined her sleeping figure and grinned to himself. This is his woman. He'd never in his 29 years, experienced sex as intense or even close to what they'd just done. Thinking about it made him feel like the biggest idiot for almost settling for someone other than her. No words could describe what this woman did to him and made him feel; she was an enigma that only he would get to solve.

Climbing into bed next to her, he draped the covers across their waists and pulled her into him rubbing her back in soothing circles. He mulled over her features trying to memorize every lash and line. This was the first time anyone's ever made him feel so at peace. He couldn't ever let her go.

Within minutes he had fallen asleep next to the woman who'd already become his everything.

JJ x

Chapter 9 - Unmoving and Awkward

- -

A lesha

I lay on my stomach, using my arms as an extra pillow as the sunlight peeked through my eyelids. Last night had to be the best night's sleep I've ever had. Having Christian next to me gave me this unfamiliar sense of safety and comfort that I knew was sure to be a new-found addiction.

"Some people would be uncomfortable with you just laying there watching them like you're doing to me right now."

I could hear him scoff, making me smile. My eyes were still shut but I could feel his gaze roaming over my bare skin. The soothing rubs from my shoulder to my lower back coupled with the light pecks he left along my arm and neck was more than enough to tempt me into spending the day right here.

"Well then it's a good thing I don't care about other people. Are you 'uncomfortable'?" He mocked.

"... Nope. I like having all your attention. I'll take your stares while I can get them."

"Good, cause I don't think I'll ever get enough. That's a promise. And this.." he said slapping my ass "is definitely not something I can keep my eyes off of."

I rolled onto my side to face him as he roped his arm around my waist pulling our naked bodies against one-another. I could feel the heat of his body, the rhythm of his heartbeat against my chest, everything. EVERY-THING.

Looking into my eyes, a sly grin appeared on his face and instantly I knew it was because of all the dirty thoughts bouncing around his head.

"Don't get any ideas buddy, you promised your brother you'd hang out with him today."

"He won't mind if I cancel. He's seen you, I'm sure he'll understand when I say I want to spend a little extra here with you instead."

"Nooo slick talker, we're going. I wanted to hang out with you guys and hear some more about the secret black brother I never knew you had."

He smiled knowing exactly what I meant.

"Secret? What are you talking about? I've talked about Demetri before."

"Yeah you've just never mentioned that he was adopted, so I always just imagined a younger version of you or Raf. When did your folks adopt him?"

"He is a younger version of me and Raf, just a different skin tone. Gramps found him 16 years ago, he was only a year old. Pops was on a job and after everything went down and they were clearing the house, he found pup hidden in a box in a room at the back of the house. He brought him home and that was it. I was only 13, it had been 3 years since my parents were taken out and I was acting like a shithead, so the minute Gramps got home he sat me down and told me I needed to clean up my act if I was gonna help him raise both my brothers, take care of Grams and eventually take over. After that talk, no-one could rip me from that boys side. Taking care of him was a way to prove myself to Gramps but I ended up just loving having another baby brother."

"You're just a big ole teddy bear in designer clothes aren't you." I joked as he kissed my forehead and nose. "What do you mean your parents were 'taken out' and what kinda house was your grandfather in to find a baby in a box?"

His face dropped as if he'd just told me something he wasn't supposed to. He quickly plastered on a fake smile before trying to piece together his next few words. "There's a lot I have to tell you but just-"

The doorbell rang , putting an end to our conversation.. for now. He groaned rolling out of the warm bed, pulling on a pair of sweats from a layer of clothes I just realized were spread at the foot of the bed. The doorbell rang again coupled with a few loud bangs on the door. Christian lightly jogged out of the room and a few seconds later I could hear as the door opened and familiar voices boomed throughout the stilled house.

Getting up from the bed I'm immediately reminded of what went down last night. The soreness around my waist, between my legs and all over my thighs was no joke. Even areas on my ribs were sensitive to the touch. I sat back down for a minute trying to ready myself for the agony again.

Mustering up the strength, I made my way to the bathroom where I saw myself in the mirror. How the hell have I been cuddled up under this man looking like a troll this whole time and he didn't say nothing?! My hair resembled a birds nest, I only thank God I wore such little makeup last night and it wasn't smudged across my face. On the counter-top he'd laid out a few things for me including a washcloth, toothbrush and a spindly little hairbrush: which he probably asked one of his guys to buy from the dollar store this morning. Bless his heart.

After brushing my teeth, I turned to the shower, it took me a good 5 minutes fiddling with the faucet to even get the shower head on. I hated using things at Chris' places, they were always too complex. I've told him before that this is what happens when rich people don't have anything to do, they make something to do.

When I got out, I tried combing my hair but, just as I guessed, broke the brush within the first 4 strokes. It wasn't even enough for a cute messy bun, I was gonna have to rock her shady sister, the tangled bun.

Walking back into the room I throw on the t-shirt and pair of boxers left on the bed before making my way to the noise downstairs. Standing in the kitchen were Christian, Demetri, Antoni and Sebastian. I walked in and all eyes were trained on me. Unmoving and awkward.

"Morning guys. When you all finish staring can somebody please point me to the orange juice?"

The boys pulled out of their stare and chuckled, each sending me a 'good morning'. Sebastian pulled a glass from the cupboard and slid it over to Antoni who poured out some juice. Christian picked it up, walking over to me. I reached my arm out but he kept the glass in his hand and brought his face closer to me speaking low enough so only I could hear.

"What are you wearing?"

"Boxers and a t-shirt. Is this a game?... What are you wearing?"

"Ha ha very funny." He deadpanned with a playful tone. "Why are you enticing my guys?"

"I didn't know asking for orange juice did that, next time I'll ask for water."
I said reaching my arm out to grab the juice, but my tiny limbs could only
stretch so far as he held the glass above his head.

"I hope you're this mouthy later when I'm ready to put it to good use,
smart-ass."

I sent him a smile dripping in sarcasm which he returned with a quick kiss
and my orange juice.

"Go get dressed we've gotta stop off at your place so you can change before
we head out."

I downed my juice and handed him the glass before heading back upstairs.
On my way up, I'm distracted when there's a knock at the front door. The
boys were too loud to have heard it so I go to answer instead. I swing open
the door and I'm greeted with a face I'm sure I knew from somewhere. The
woman motions to walk past me but I push the door closed a little more
so it's only cracked open slightly.

"Can I help you?"

I ask in my most polite voice. She opens her mouth but before she can say
anything all four boys come rushing in our direction, Christian shouting
in a panic.

"Alesha get away from the door! Who is that?!"

Without waiting for an answer he grabs my arm pulling me back beside
him causing the door to swing open. Seeing the pretty blonde he lets out a
relieved sigh, but his grip on my arm is still firm.

"What the fuck do you want Charlotte?"

JJ x

Chapter 10 - I Know

Christian

I won't lie, seeing how she got the boys' attention aggravated my jealous side. I don't care where they gawk as long as it's not at her. At least we were leaving soon so telling her to go get dressed gave me time to let the boys know where they stood. She left to head back upstairs and I turned to Toni and Seb.

"You guys have a good stare?"

Demetri raised a brow, shook his head and turned to the bowl of cereal in front of him.

Antoni and Sebastian looked to each other trying to decipher the right thing to say. Seeing them flustered made me bust out laughing, they joined in with a sigh of relief. I wasn't seriously worried about them making any moves on my girl, they've seen me do worse for less, but even then I don't want them looking too close. "Seriously, don't." I deadpanned

We were about to go back to planning out the day when Demetri spoke up.

"Wasn't that the front door just now?"

"What are you talking about?" I grabbed one of my guns from under the sink and left the kitchen as the boys followed with their own weapons in hand. Stepping into the hall I see Alesha standing at the unlocked door, talking through the cracked opening. A mixture of fear and anger surged through my body. An unexpected visitor is never a good thing when it comes to the people I know.

"Alesha get away from the door! Who is that?!"

I sprint over to her ready for anything. I gripped her upper arm and pulled her beside me and took a step in front of her. I didn't clock she still had a hold on the door handle so when I yanked her, it came swinging open too. Gun ready by my side, I saw the face causing all this unease. As much as I hate her, I was grateful it wasn't someone more malignant. Then again...

"What the fuck do you want Charlotte?"

The boys rolled their eyes making their way back to the kitchen, already knowing she was most likely about to cause some drama. Before walking back, Seb covertly took my gun so Alesha wouldn't see it.

Oh shit, Alesha. I was too caught up in the possibility of something happening to her, I didn't realize how harsh my grip was. I finally looked down to her sweet face only to see she was a little rattled. I quickly release my clutch on her arm knowing I fucked up. I open my mouth to apologize and instead I'm brought back to the fact I have a headache to handle.

"You know, I love it when you make a fuss over me schmoopy. You should get a new maid though, this one wouldn't let me in; almost scuffed my YSL pumps, these are the ones you got me for my birthday too."

That fucking pet name and the baby voice makes me wish Seb hadn't taken my gun.

"Charlotte, I'll only tell you this once, watch your mouth, especially when it comes to her." I point behind me to A. "Don't come back here and make me do something you'll regret."

"Dammit Christian! I just wanted to talk to you about the charity auction on the 16th."

"A month from now? What about it?"

"I found the perfect dress to go flawlessly with your blue tux. Be at my place by 8, I want to get there early, I heard that bitch Nina Westbrooke wants to outbid me for the 19th century Monet so daddy and I need to have a little talk with the auctioneer beforehand."

"Your best friend Nina?"

"Yes. So meet me at my place 8 sharp."

"What about our situation makes you think I'll be doing any of that?"

Before she could say anything, I felt myself reach the limit of what I could tolerate and I slammed the door in her face.

Now she was done with, I turned around with my apology ready for Alesha, but she was gone. I didn't even hear her walk away. I thought I fucked up before, there was no question about it now. I made my way upstairs knowing that's most likely where she went.

Getting to the bedroom I see her folding my t-shirt, already changed into her dress from last night and I can't help but feel like a piece of shit when I see a bruise forming on her arm. She must've heard me come in the room because she started talking with her back turned.

"You know, I thought I recognized her. She was the model at my shoot yesterday, looked shocked when I mentioned you. Knowing your past I should've put 2 and 2 together."

"Baby, I'm so sorry. I didn't mean to grab you like that."

"Why were you even freaking out?"

"I just- I wasn't expecting anyone other than the guys and I got a little overprotective."

Turning around she let out a scoff, shaking her head at me in disbelief. "I know there's something you're not telling me. Ever since I met you, there's been something off and I chose to ignore it and play the fool because 'the cute guy makes me laugh and I'm happy with him' but I'm done. I don't know if it's because you don't trust me or what. It's like you've got this second side that I never see. Well, it ends now, you either tell me the truth or we go our separate ways. Your choice."

Her calmness was eerie. I looked at her unable to say anything because the lies won't come quick enough and even if they did, I don't think I could, not to her. Taking my silence as an answer she gave me a nod, grabbed her shoes, jacket and purse and headed for the door. I stepped in front of it blocking her exit, hoping she would change her mind.

"Babe come on. Just take a minute and relax."

"I am relaxed. Christian it's fine, you've made your decision and now I'm making mine."

It felt like everything was moving at a distorted pace and I couldn't stop her, so I did the only thing I could think to make her stay.

"I'm head of the Italian mafia."

She could probably see my heart hammering against my chest the thing was beating so hard. Waiting for her reaction put my nerves on edge. She took a deep breath and sighed.

"I know."

JJ x

Chapter 11 - Meltdowns and Freakouts

C hristian

"You know? What do you mean you know?"

"How could I not know about the illustrious Marino family? I've been waiting years to take you down and I've finally gotten you all alone."

I just stood there, speechless. I was being played this entire time? I'd taken every cautionary measure I could. My heart was beating like a jackhammer and wouldn't let up. How the fuck did I let this happen?!

"Holy shit, baby I'm kidding. Do you wanna sit down? You look like you're about to pass out."

She dropped her things to the floor and rushed over, leading me to the couch at the other end of the room. I was still processing her cruel joke as she coolly flopped down next to me. "Did you really know?" She nod her head, while casually using her hands to fan me down. "How did you know?"

"Danielle told me. Over a phone call. In the middle of the night. After she found out from Rafael."

I put her hands in mine to stop the erratic fanning that got more aggressive as she explained. "I'm sorry. Raf wasn't supposed to say anything."

"What do you think I'm mad about right now? Because Rafael ain't it. It's the fact that I'm hearing things about you second-hand. It doesn't matter if it's from my best friend or my worst enemy, you should've let me know from the jump."

"Trust me, I get that, but this one isn't just a regular white lie. I promise though, it won't happen again."

"Better not. Must think I'm playing with you." She mumbled under her breath, purposely clear enough for me to hear. "I mean I had my suspicions about what you actually did for a living but I should've known. To be honest it was either something illegal or a secret family no-one knew about. Since we met you've always acted shady with the 'private family business', leaving dinners early, taking mysterious phone calls you didn't want me to hear, then yesterday I noticed Sebastian following me, but what really brought it home were the guns. You know I'm not blind, right?"

"Your little act wasn't funny, I could've killed you."

"Would that have been before or after you passed out, Mr. Mafia? You were turning so pale, looked like you'd seen a ghost."

I let out an alleviated laugh as my heart finally started returning to a less frenzied pace. She looked at me with an amused smile that slowly started to fade, bringing my laughter to a stop.

"Were you ever going to tell me? I mean if I hadn't threatened to walk out, would you have told me?"

"Honestly? I promised myself I would after I locked you down." I say trying to lighten her mood, but she still looked hurt, presumably knowing what else I was about to say. "But no, I don't think I would've. I love how you look at me like I could do no wrong. When it's me and you, it's just us, there's no worries about shipments or double crossing or looking over my shoulder. Meeting you was hands down the best thing to happen to me. I don't think I was ready to let that go. I'm still not."

She chuckled running a hand through my hair to soothe me, leaning into her touch I look into those honey brown irises that weaken me so easily.

"I haven't looked at you any differently and I promise to keep it that way, as long as you end it with the secrets."

"Why aren't you losing your shit and flipping out? Have you got any idea what I've done since joining this organization? What could have happened to you if it wasn't Charlotte downstairs and someone worse?"

"I'm new to this so no, I didn't know opening the door could've killed me. And yes I did have a little meltdown this morning after the phone call, but I was laying there next to you and it's kind of hard to see some monster when I'm looking at this face." She placed a peck on my lips. "Besides your Gramps told me something last night and I need to believe what he said is true. I think I know the part of you that matters, I definitely trust you and I lo- I got over the idea of the 'big bad wolf' pretty fast."

"You're not scared knowing what it means to be wife of the capo?"

"I don't know what it means and I'm not your wife."

"Not yet."

"That's if Stacey doesn't get her way with you, she's a dedicated thottie. Determined to be a side chick turned main chick, or die trying."

"What's a Stacey?"

"You don't remember Miss 'call me, we'd have a lot of fun together.'" She put on an airy breathless tone mocking the girl.

It wasn't too far off. "The other receptionist, Diane, told me how she was trying to get with you, I don't know how badly you bruised her ego, but after you came to see me at the office, she started a rumor that I was sleeping my way to the top with one of the company's millionaire investors."

"I mean, I haven't offered you a promotion or given you a raise.. at this point you're just sleeping with one of the billionaire investors."

Pinching the bridge of her nose, she sighed exasperated.

"Am I the only one in this entire city that doesn't know who the hell you are?"

"That's funny, because I think you're the only one who does. You got to know me pretty well last night, if that wasn't enough you can get to know me a little better right now."

I smirked as I swung her leg over my lap so she was straddling me. Trailing kisses from my lips to my neck, she nibbled on my earlobe, her warm tongue and cool breath making every inch of me stand at attention.

Sliding my hands up her thighs to her hips, I can tell she's not wearing any underwear under her dress and I feel myself stiffen as she slowly grazed her warm slit against my sweats, the relentless grinding had me letting out deep guttural groans. "You have no fucking idea what you do to me."

"Are y'all almost ready to go-"

Demetri walked in and all movement stopped. Alesha dropped her head against my shoulder while I glared at him.

"Why are you still here?! Get out!"

"Chris, stop. Don't worry, we're coming now." Alesha spoke unsteadily.

"Yeah I could see that. Y'all so nasty, you got people downstairs." He replied chuckling.

"Get the fuck out!"

Once he left the room, Alesha broke into a soft giggle. "It was fun while it lasted."

"This is definitely not over."

She got up from my lap making my mood deflate completely. I held onto her hand before she could walk away, just one thing I needed to know.

"Would you have really left?"

"Never."

JJ x

Chapter 12 - The 1%

- -

A lesha

It was already the Saturday of the charity auction and we've managed to get by a month without any more drama from ex girlfriends. Y'all know what bitch I'm talking about. I've been looking forward to this dinner all week. Since Charlotte had nerve to stop by the house and demand Christian be her date, he figured there was no better way to make us official and put an end to her than taking me instead.

After being talked into cashing in some of my unused vacation days, we spent all of this week under one another, but I needed a break. Since we got together he hasn't let me go, I was walking around like a pimp with a bad limp for a good few days.

I only got away long enough to go dress hunting then for lunch with Dani. Only my best friend could leave everything to the last minute and still end up finding something one of a kind and drop dead gorgeous. After dropping her off at her and Raf's apartment, I headed back to my place to pick up my dress, then I was straight back to Christian's to get ready.

Walking through the front door I'm hit with the scent of his cologne, I love that freaking smell. Stood in the foyer, he was in a heated conversation with whoever was on the other end of the call. My eyes could only focus on his body and how handsome he looked, dressed in a crisp black tuxedo that clung perfectly to every inch of his skin. He spoke with a roughness in his tone making him even sexier. I just wanted to- wait... is that Russian?

"Она не вовлечена в это. Я хочу Васильева. Приведи его ко мне... живым. Найти его. СЕЙЧАС!"(She is not involved in this. I want Vasiliev. Bring him to me... alive. Find him. NOW!)

He moved the phone from his ear, ending the call with a scowl etched on his face.

"What's got you so pissed? Were you speaking Russian just now?"

He looked up surprised to see me standing at the door, his expression relaxed into a warm smile as he made his way over to me, gently tugging me into him. He captured my lips in a sweet kiss before pulling away leaving me wanting more.

"Don't worry about that. This the dress?"

He pointed to the garment bag hanging off my pointer finger.

"Yeah. I'm pretty excited about this dinner. In college I used to volunteer at the women's shelter this charity works with, you have no idea how much this money's gonna help them."

"Everyday I learn something new about you." He started trailing his lips down my neck until finding his favourite spot on my collar bone.

"How do we donate anyway? Is it gonna be like a donation box? Is this an offering bag situation or what?"

He pulled his head back and chuckled lightly, amused by my questions.

"Babe that's not how these people do charity events. The donation money's collected from the tickets."

"Okay, so how much should I bring for the tickets?"

"They're 15 a plate and have already been bought. You know I hate you using your money if you don't have to. I have enough to spare for shit like this."

"Christian, please not again." I trailed off dismissively not wanting to have this conversation for the umpteenth time. "If these dinners are only 15 bucks why is it only the rich and famous that get the invites?"

"You're adorable, you know that? It's 15 thousand." He said nonchalantly.

My eyes widened and I'm pretty sure my jaw is hitting the floor. They're all really about to spend that much money to dress up, drink champagne and eat small portions of decorative food? "I'm sure they'd help a lot more if they scrap the expensive wine and barely-there food and just give all the money to the shelter."

"It's more about keeping up appearances than it is about the actual charities." He shrugged and I couldn't help the look of slight disgust that showed on my face at how indifferently the words left him.

"I'm not saying it's a good thing, I'm just saying it's a thing. Plus, our family charities that Grams manage, more than make up for the shambles these guys claim to invest in."

Yet again, he's redeemed. Is it bad when you don't notice any negative traits in your partner? It has to be, right? No one can be perfect, it's not possible, yet this man right here checks all the right boxes. Or it might just be that since finding out about his actual 9-5, I've been putting off learning the ins and outs of it all, scared to know what he's done and who he is outside of being my Chris.

I'm asking him to tell me everything. Tonight. After the dinner. I just don't know if I'm ready to learn what kind of things the man I'm in love with is truly capable of, but I'm gonna find out.Wait.. In love with?!HmmmI love him.

Feeling a slight unease at how vulnerable I felt using that word, I tried distancing myself from him, but his grip on my waist tightened.

"I have to get ready."

I pushed my way out of his hold and started running upstairs feeling his eyes latched on my every step.

"Stop staring at my butt!"

"It's my butt too now."

He ain't lying.

JJ x

Chapter 13 - I'm Only Okay If You're Okay

C hristian

Laying across the bed I replied to texts as I waited for Alesha to finish her makeup in the bathroom so we could get going to this stupid 'whose wallet's thicker' dinner which admittedly couldn't have come at a better time, I needed a distraction. This fall through deal with the Russians had been kicking my ass.

Ivan Vasiliev, the head of the Bratva, took offense to my rejection of his terms, so he's put a minor hit out on me, which in our business can make a lot of smaller men feel brave. If anything I'm insulted, I'm sure I'm worth more than $7B. Had he stopped there I would've happily only wiped out his men to teach him a lesson, but earlier when Ethan called, he told me that Ivan somehow found out about Alesha. They don't know everything, just enough to know she's a good target to shoot for.

I'm gonna have fun torturing him.

I'm taken out of my thoughts and sit up when I hear the bathroom door open. Stepping into the bedroom, my eyes scour her entire body in that dress.

Wow.

The green silk hugged her creamy deep brown skin as she made her way over to the floor length mirror checking each angle in her reflection.

The word beautiful doesn't do her justice.

"What do you think? Maybe I should've taken up your offer of a new dress instead of wearing one of my college projects. It's nothing like the designer dresses the other women are gonna be wearing."

I got up making my way behind her, wrapping my arms around her waist. A sudden thirst washes over me as I'm mesmerized by her reflection.

"I don't care what they'll be wearing, I'm just worried other guys won't be able to stop staring at you. You look stunning baby. Plus, it's a one of a kind, like you."

"God, you're so cheesy." She blushed leaning her head back into my chest.

"I can't help it.. you're perfect."

***

Pulling up to the museum the dinner was being held at, I looked over to Alesha. She hadn't said much since we got in the car and that threw me because I usually can't shut her up. She looked like she was deep in thought about something important.

"Are you okay? If you wanna ditch, it's not too late." I joked reaching over to brush the hair from her face. She looked up at me with a smile that didn't quite meet her eyes. I could easily tell something was on her mind. "Seriously, talk to me. What's up?" I rest my hand on her thigh with a comforting squeeze.

"Let's talk later."

"Is something wrong?"

"... I want you to tell me everything. What you've done and- just everything. Is that okay?"

I paused unsure of what to say. I don't know if I want her looking at me horrified or timid like everyone else does. If she finds out half the things I've done, well, there's no going back. I took a deep breath reminding myself that she also found out I was a mob boss and went right back to sleep next to me. Convincing myself she could handle it, I release my breath and reply.

"I'll tell you anything you wanna know."

That smile breaks out on her face. The one that reassures me she's okay, which means I'm okay. The one that wraps me around her little finger. She leans in leaving a soft kiss on my lips, staring into my eyes.

"I lo-"

A knock on the window of the car interrupted her, getting our attention. Danielle and Rafael stood on the pavement wiggling their brows and grinning at us as I rolled down the window.

"Are you two tryna get freaky in there? Oooh y'all tryna be one of them 'adventurous couples' huh." Dani teased as she held onto Rafael's arm.

"Love, don't act innocent now, up until a couple minutes ago we were having some fun of our own in the car, so what does that make us?" He 'whispered' nipping at her neck making her squirm and giggle.

"I think that's our cue to get inside. Save the sex stories for someone with a stronger stomach."

One of the valets made his way over to the car as I stepped out passing him my keys and a tip. I walked around to Alesha's door and helped her out.

"Are the others here yet?" I questioned, hoping I'd be able to avoid most of the people in there and spend the night with my family instead.

"The old timers got here earlier and pup is probably gonna make some grand entrance."

-

Walking into the brightly lit hall, Alesha couldn't help but look around stunned at the ballroom's decor. The light bounced off of the gold interior leaving everything in a glistening shadow. The hall was filled with rumbling chatter over the soft instrumental tunes coming from the band on stage. There were people in extravagant gowns and polished suits having conversations in different corners of the room.

Eyes turned to the entrance as the group walked into the hall. Rafael and Danielle were first through the doors gaining a few friendly smiles and waves, and doing the same back to the random guests.

Following them, Christian entered with Alesha locked in his arm and all the previously smiling faces dropped to ones of slight panic as if not expecting him. The guests quickly made sure to correct their expressions before nodding their heads, almost as a bow to Christian.

Alesha took no notice of the attention they were getting as she was too enthralled with the excess of her surroundings. Soon they had found Winnie and Vincenzo talking with an older couple, who Alesha could swear she recognized. The chat between the small pairings seemed stiff and a little more than uncomfortable to say the least.

"Hey Grams, Gramps. You guys really showed out tonight huh? Trying to show everybody you still got it old man?" Rafael interjected.

Their grandparents spun around to greet them, bright grins plastered on their faces.

"First of all, my wife always shows out. I'm just trying to keep up with her." Vincenzo smiled looking down at Winnie before greeting the group with hugs. Winnie tried doing the same before they were impeded by the couple from earlier who hadn't moved.

"Hello Christian, I was just telling your grandparents I'm expecting to see them and yourself at my 66th birthday celebration, I've decided to embrace aging as I saw your grandmother do at her 76th" Alesha and Dani looked surprised to not only hear she was younger than Winnie but only 65. "We were expecting you a little sooner. Charlotte had informed us you were to be arriving promptly at 8:45pm. Speaking of, where is my daughter?"

That's why they looked so familiar, they were an unfailingly perfect mixture of Charlotte. The lady spoke in a smooth, deep tone that sent uncomfortable chills down everyone's spine.

"Daughter my ass, she know that's her great grand-baby." Dani muttered loud enough for their group to hear and chuckle to.

"Richard and Regina Brunswick, meet my girlfriend Alesha Moore. Sweetheart these are Charlotte's parents."

Alesha held her hand out as the couple glared at Christian with a look of disgust and anger. They stared Christian down, ignoring Alesha's hand but Christian smirked as if he dared them to disrespect her.

Even though his lips were curled in a taunting sneer, his eyes were cold and emotionless as if bored and ready to end them right there and then. He could tell as the fear suddenly coursed through them. Richard took Alesha's hand in his sending her a nervous smile as he shook it, while Regina just turned around and walked away, her husband following shortly after.

When Demetri had arrived, the gang formed their own circle sharing jokes and catching up on everyone's week before the dinner officially began. Christian saw the way Alesha mingled with his family and he was never more sure that she was the one for him. He couldn't help but look at her in awe as she blended flawlessly into the group.

Alesha also noticed how much deeper she was being sucked into Christian's life and she cherished the feeling. For the longest time it had just been her and Dani and now she had this family of amazing people who wanted to include both of them and seemed to genuinely want them around.

She'd written people off for so long masking the fear of everyone leaving with the idea that she was better off alone, yet here he was. Just looking at him made the hairs on her skin raise. In the time they've known each other he'd quickly become the closest person to her. Dani would always be her sister but she'd now found her best friend, her other half.

She'd never told anyone she loved them, well except for Dani. Even so, that didn't happen until the 7th grade when she saved Alesha from an unnecessary cat fight by beating up a bully. The thought of giving someone that kind of power over her emotions was terrifying. The minute she thought she was going to say it earlier she ran away, in the car it was on repeat in her mind and right now, well there was no hiding from it. Whatever he told her tonight, she wasn't leaving.

"WHAT THE FUCK CHRISTIAN?!"

The whispered shriek came from behind the couple, getting the attention of their entire family.

"You didn't pick me up and I've been waiting for over 3 hours, so I repeat: What. The actual. Fuck?!"

"Oh, hey Charlotte. Sounds like you were expecting me or something."

"We discussed this! Is this you being 'petty'? I had to take an Uber here and there weren't any executive cars available so a 2003 Honda Civic was my only option. Do you know how disgusting and inconvenient that was?"

"Almost as disgusting and inconvenient as turning up to an ex's house, disrespecting his girlfriend and demanding he caters to you."

Everyone turned to Dani, who looked up casually from playing with her nails.

"What? My best friend might have too much class to check you, but don't let it happen with me around, cause I'm always ready."

Raf licked his lips looking at Dani hungrily. Charlotte sent Dani an exaggeratedly fake smile turning her rant back to Christian.

"Having these people see me arrive in that... monstrosity was one thing, but having to turn up alone? Christian I have never been so embarrassed. I never arrive single."

"Aww hun, if you show up wearing this but insist the most embarrassing part of your night is turning up alone, I would suggest you rethink your priorities." Winnie stated taking a sip from her glass of champagne.

"I'd have you know Winifred, this is couture straight from the runway."

"Little girl, when you saw it, you should've run away. You know, Alesha has a real job working for a fashion company, even made the beautiful dress she's wearing tonight. If you've got some free time from all your heiress-ing you could go to her office and learn a few things. You come from too much money to be leaving the house like this."

Winnie walked away with her grinning husband in tow, his arm draped around her waist, placing a kiss on her temple.

-

The rest of the night went perfectly, apart from the vexed glares from Charlotte and her folks which Alesha tried to ignore, and the 'discreet' lust-filled stares aimed at Alesha which Christian curbed with a warning scowl.

They figured it was time to say their goodbyes after Raf's flirty glances at Dani turned into an unashamedly loud 25 minute "bathroom break".

They were in the car headed back to the house and were both pretty sure the talk was going to wait until they had some loud fun of their own. The whole car ride Christian's hand massaged the smooth skin of Alesha's inner thigh, teasing close enough to her centre that her breathing was a little heavier than usual. She rested her hand on the nape of his neck playing in his hair and avoiding eye contact; she knew if he could see how much she wanted him right now, they wouldn't make it back to the house.

Christian opened the front door to the eerily quiet home. He was slightly apprehensive due to the pitch black scenery; he's never come home to a dark house unless he'd been away for long periods of time.

He turned the light switch on, only to see Ivan leaning on the rail at the top of the stairs and a little over what seemed like 30 of his men perched randomly on the imperial staircase, all with guns in hand, pointed at them.

He forcefully tucked Alesha halfway behind him, clutching her hip to keep her in place.

"DeLuca! Добро пожаловать домой. Я слышал, что ты искал меня, поэтому я решил, почему бы не прийти к вам."(Welcome home. I heard that you were looking for me, so I decided, why not come to you.)

"What the fuck do you think you're pulling here Vasiliev?" Chris demanded an answer through gritted teeth. Alesha could feel the heat radiating off of him. This was beyond simple anger, this was a growing rage.

Ivan spoke in a thick Russian accent. "Oh, don't get shy on me now Christian. I see you've brought company along too." His focus turned to Alesha. "Look at you in that dress. Mr Marino you really do have all the luck, don't you. Those pictures did not do you justice little one, I'll admit I still had fun with them. I was hoping the real thing would live up to my imagination." He took a step back cocking his gun. "But then again, I think I'd prefer seeing your boyfriend suffer."

He pulled the trigger and as Christian attempted to shield Alesha, he heard the familiar clear but faint whistling of the silencer.

JJ x

Chapter 14 - Vasiliev's Army

A lesha

I felt Christian's grip on my hip tighten as he turned trying to shield me. I closed my eyes waiting for the pain to set in. Nothing. Peeking through my lids, I opened my eyes one at a time to Christian facing me, a look of relief mixed with growing fury clouded his expression. Did this... Vaseline guy actually just shoot at me or am I freaking out to the point of hearing and seeing things?

"You know Vasiliev, I underestimated you. You must have some big ass fucking balls to break in here and not only threaten me but her. Of all the people you could've gone after, really?" Christian spoke enraged with his eyes tightly shut before calmly opening them to mine. "I really hope you know how this ends for you. At least you'll get to die with your men here by your side."

"At least my men have yet to turn on me. I should remember to thank Mr Howard for letting us in tonight. Marino, the more you talk, the more I want to break you down to nothing, til you're begging for me to stop. You were right to take the bullet, thank you; your wife will have more fun being ripped apart by my men and I before killing her, all while you watch."

His "take the bullet" comment had me scanning Christian's body looking for a wound, but he wasn't bleeding. It was only then that the man's words started settling in, along with my panic.

"After that show, I can't imagine there will be much more breaking to be done before killing you too. I can't promise you'll have as good a time as I will. Отведи их в спальню. Убей его, если придется, но она мне нужна живьем. Она получит прощальный трах, которого она действительно заслуживает."(Take them to the bedroom. Kill him if you have to, but I need her alive. She will get the farewell fuck she really deserves.)

I didn't know what he said but Vasiliev broke into a sadistic grin as his men all started chuckling loudly. My eyes were glued to them as they started walking down the stairs toward us, their guns lazily trained on Christian's back. Their stares were disturbing, raking over my body. I was oblivious to how deep my nails were digging into Christian's waist and the tears spilling from my eyes until he lifted his hand wiping my face.

"Don't worry about them. Look at me. Nothing will happen to you."

I nodded my head, staring into his eyes. He smiled back at me, but it wasn't his usual charming, endearing smile. It was one I'd never seen on him before, this one was devilish almost identical to the one Vasiliev wore. The attraction I felt earlier was now being smothered with a growing fear.

He raised a brow turning to the men who had now made their way directly behind him and were reaching out to grab his shoulders. The deep red seeping through his white dress shirt caught my eye. He was shot, the wound kept pumping out blood, leaving a trail straight from his shoulder blade down to his waist.

As soon as one of the men had their hand on his shoulder, Christian grabbed his wrist, pushing back on his palm until there were crisp snapping sounds signaling his hand was broken. It happened so fast no-one was able to gauge what took place till the man's roaring scream tore through the halls.

In the blink of an eye Christian had snatched his gun and was shooting off automatic rounds. The bullets were slicing through different parts of every man. Tearing through arms, legs, throats and heads. My mind was shouting for me to run for safety and do anything but stand watching all this go down, but I couldn't, my dumb-ass legs stood still.

Every single man was on the floor letting out painful pleas and groans as they bled to death while Christian pulled a knife from the jacket of his first victim and plunged it into his chest over and over and over again. Once he lay on the floor lifeless, Christian proceeded to tend to the others, echoing the same merciless blows to their chests until there was a screeching silence. By the time he was done, there wasn't an inch of his body not covered in the blood of the men strewn all over the marble floor.

This was nothing like in the movies. There were pieces of limbs everywhere and heads practically severed from corpses. The sounds of their screams and shrieks were haunting and the squelch of the knife passing through their flesh pierced my eardrums. Not to mention the smell, it was instantaneous. It smelt like an unusual combination of rotting vomit and metal.

I shuddered out of my trance when I heard a loud boisterous laugh like that of a lunatic.

"IVAN! COME ON DOWN, COME SEE WHAT I'VE DONE TO YOUR MEN! IT'S BEEN A WHILE SINCE I'VE TAKEN PART IN THAT KIND OF ENTERTAINMENT, I'VE MISSED IT! CAN'T WAIT TO SEE HOW LONG YOU HOLD OUT WHILE I SKIN YOU ALIVE!"

His chest was rising and falling at a pace that let me know the adrenaline was still surging through his veins. His screams to the empty house came to a halt when he noticed me standing in the same spot. I wonder if he can see the terror in my eyes, because I only just realized how violently my body was shaking.

Christian

I didn't know what to do. Her whole body was shaking uncontrollably. Her eyes stapled wide in disbelief, red from the streams of tears flooding her face. I stepped forward with outstretched arms wanting to hold and comfort her but seeing that my usual ivory toned arms were slathered in a crimson hue, with a gun and knife still in hand, I changed my mind. Doesn't mean I was oblivious to her flinch as I moved toward her.

She's scared of me.

I was straight back in defense mode when I heard the front door open. Antoni and Sebastian came walking in.

"Boss we just s..."

Without hesitation I put a bullet in his head. Fucking traitor.

JJ x

Chapter 15 - Your World

Alesha

It's been nearly a month since that night. I spent the first week, in my apartment away from everyone and everything. By week 2 I was back at work but still skittish at loud sounds and sudden movements. I couldn't sleep, my mind was recycling nightmares and images of those men. I haven't been able to get any of it out of my head. I haven't been able to get him out of my head.

I couldn't find words to say to him, so I avoided his frequent calls and ignored his incessant visits with relentless knocks and pleads at my door. I wasn't mad at him or scared, he just didn't seem the same, especially after our talk.

~

There was a ringing in my ear and my eyes were stuck on a blood drenched Christian. My stare followed as his attention turned behind me to the front door. Within seconds of recognizing Antoni and Sebastian, my heart drops straight into my gut at the loud *BANG*.

Sebastian's head shattered, leaving droplets of brain matter splattered on the wall and floor behind him. I looked wide eyed between Christian's extended arm holding the gun and the additional dead body missing a face before settling on the latter. I was in so much shock I didn't notice Antoni moving until his hand reached up to wipe something off my cheek. Pulling his hand away, I see it matches the muck that was seeping from Sebastian's head.

I walked quickly to the bathroom making sure to avoid stepping on any of the massacred corpses or the liquids oozing from them. Getting in the bathroom, I lock the door and rush over to the toilet. Everything I ate that evening was coming out in uncontrollable spews. My throat burned from the vomit but even with an empty stomach, my body was still dry heaving looking for anything to expel.

After a while, I got up and washed out my mouth before taking my place back in front of the toilet bowl. I sat there for what felt like only a minute until I felt a hand on my shoulder. I looked up to see Antoni again looking at me with apologetic eyes. A worried Christian stood behind him next to the broken bathroom door.

Antoni leaned into my face dragging my attention to him, I could see his lips moving but couldn't hear him, everything was coming out in drowned murmurs. He helped me onto my feet and guided me upstairs. I felt numb.

Steam rose from the water filled tub. Antoni's words started getting clearer as he walked around the bathroom collecting a few things.

"-shot so close to you. I never liked Sebastian, but I don't know how Julian Howard will take the news of Christian killing his son. The muffled hearing should be going by now, can you hear me?" He stopped moving around long enough to watch me nod. "Hopefully he didn't frighten you breaking the door down like that, but I think he nearly popped the veins in his head when you weren't answering."

He hung everything on the hooks next to the tub as he continued. "A, I know it's a lot to take in but you've gotta know he didn't mean for you to be part of any of that. I can't imagine what it'd be like if Rochelle found out what I do for a living; she'd blow my fucking brains ou-" He stopped himself.

...

"He loves you, you know that." His eyes and soft smile still held that 'I'm sorry' look. "I've gotta call the cleanup crew. You just have a bath and try to take a nap, I doubt you'll be able to, but you need some rest. Just whatever you do, don't come downstairs. I'll come get you when it's clear." With that he left.

I tried relaxing and taking the bath, but it wasn't enough, I needed to scrub tonight off of me. I got in the shower and scrubbed until my skin was sore and it still didn't feel like I washed it all away.

After I got out of the shower and brushed my teeth I just wanted to go home. I put on a pair of gray sweats and a white t-shirt with some sneakers and sat on the edge of the bed waiting for Antoni to come tell me it was okay to leave. I could hear Christian's hushed frantic whispers coming from outside. I walked to the door pressing the side of my head against it, trying to ear hustle.

"How was she? Does she need anything? Has she said anything yet? Does she still look scared?"

"Boss calm down. She's gonna need some time for all this to settle, but I think she'll be okay. She's not talking yet but she's also not freaking out. What she needs is for those bodies to be as far away from her as possible, which I will handle.. but you man; she might not feel like it yet, but she needs you. Maybe just tidy up a little first, best she doesn't see you like this."

-

It was 3:45am and I was still sitting in the same spot on the bed. I'd turned the lights out because the brightness was starting to hurt my eyes. I felt tired but I couldn't bring myself to keep my eyes shut for very long. My mind was on a constant loop of the evening. I'm out of my depth and not prepared for any of this.

Christian stepped into the room in a fresh pair of black sweats and t-shirt, he walked across the room, taking a seat in the armchair to the corner and resting his head in his hands. He let out a deep sigh before starting.

"Baby, I'm so sorry you had to see any of that. It's not something that should've happened, and I swear to God I'll make sure it never will again."

Hearing him talk about it made my mind run through the night's events. I completely forgot that he was shot! I got up rushing over to him. He looked up as I stood in front of him motioning for him to lean forward, I pulled his shirt up noticing the gash was now covered with a bandage.

"I'm fine. Toni stitched me up." He hugged my waist burying his head into my stomach and I couldn't help but feel a wave of relief that he was okay and seemed back to normal. Still, this isn't something I can go through again. I know he said there wouldn't be a repeat, but there's only so much you can promise when this is your life.

"Christian I'm so sorry, but I need to go." I said in a voice barely above a whisper.

I kissed the top of his head and pulled out of his hold. He looked at me with pure confusion stirring in his green eyes and said nothing.

I was already at the door reaching out for the handle when he finally spoke.

"Alesha, where do you think you're going?" he asked in a deep and unsettling tone.

"I just saw you commit mass murder Christian. I can't be a part of this world, your world. I'm not built for this life, if this is who you are then.." I let out a humorless chuckle. "I couldn't stomach today let alone the rest of my life. I need to leave, and you need to let me." My voice was so low, even breaking toward the end. Each word provoked tears to spill from my eyes and even more came rushing when I could see how what I said must've felt like daggers to his chest.

"You can either stay and talk to me or calm down outside and we'll talk when you're ready, but you are NOT leaving me." His once sexy, endearing voice turned cold and sent frightening shivers throughout my body and I don't know who was staring back at me, but I could no longer see my Christian, not the man I love.

"I can't stay. If you need to hate me that's okay, I should've thought it through before jumping into this." At this point I could feel the tears seeping through my t-shirt and onto my chest. "I love you b-"

"YOU DO NOT GET TO SAY THAT THEN TURN AND WALK THE FUCK OUT!" The bass and volume in his voice shook my core. I've never seen him like this, this angry.

"Goodbye Christian." I picked up my purse, keys and the bag holding my dress and shoes. I left the room and got to the garage. Driving away from his house all I could feel was regret. I wanted to turn around and go be with him. I just couldn't.

~

"Hey, you paying attention? Where do you wanna go out for dinner tonight? I beg of you no more seafood. I'm pretty sure you had me eat the entire ocean this week." Richard and I were sat at a cute little restaurant in a quiet town just outside Paris.

We'd been in France almost 2 weeks for Fashion Week and it's just the break I needed. He'd also noticed how differently I've been behaving, so suggested we stay an extra week to relax after the shows were done.

"Actually, if you're up for it Danielle and her beau should be landing in a few hours, we can grab some dinner with them?"

"That sounds great, I haven't seen her since the whole Chris and Liam fiasco."

"She's said not to bring it up anymore. It was your fault anyway. You know how she is, but the minute you get the Hemsworth brothers as clients you invite her to the office to meet them? Rookie move Dunkirk."

"You're right I'll take blame for that one. I just didn't expect one person to have so many sexual jokes and innuendos at the ready."

We finished our lunch and went around the small-town sightseeing before heading back to the hotel.

I'd texted Dani and Raf telling them which restaurant to meet us at. Richard and I got there early and decided to open the wine while we waited. We were chatting and laughing when out of the corner of my eye I spotted Dani.

Richard and I stood up getting ready to hug her. She looked nervous as she walked over. She pulled Richard in for a hug while I tilted my head smiling a little confused.

"Hey, where's Raf?"

"I didn't know he was coming, don't hate me."

"What are you talking about?"

I looked back to the entrance and smiled as I saw Rafael walk in. The grin was gone just as fast as Christian followed behind him.

JJ x

Chapter 16 - Being Greater

C hristian

We sat on the sofa, her legs resting in my lap as I kneaded into the soles of her feet and she replied to work emails on her laptop. I would usually try to get out of masseur duty by whining, making jokes about her feet stinking or something, but today was different. She's been a little stressed after getting a phone call from her mom asking for money. With promises of a foot rub and pizza, I'd just gotten her to calm down after a very long, very loud rant.

She stops typing and looks to the ceiling holding her pointer finger in the air next to her head. "You know what's funny?" I'm pretty sure that's rhetorical so I keep my mouth shut and do my job. "Instead of raising me, like a real mother would, she made me raise myself and now expects me to take care of her. Unbelievable!"

She rolled her eyes throwing her head back as her hand came down slapping her thigh. I reach my arms up rubbing her legs as if it reassured her that I understood her frustration. A few seconds pass without her saying anything and I hear a sniffle before she starts speaking in a whispered tone.

"You know she didn't even ask how I was. I haven't seen or spoken to my mother in almost 7 years and the first thing she says is "I need $6000". I shouldn't be upset, I'm used to this version of Esther. It's not like she's been a mom. She gave up on that a long time ago. I woke myself up and made my own lunches for school, I sat by myself at parent/teacher meetings making excuses for her, I took up paper rounds to buy shit I needed. Hell, I put myself through college to start a career I'm proud of. Telling me I should be thankful for all she's done?! I'm nothing but a joke to her, so fucking stupid."

I closed the laptop and put it on the coffee table. Gripping under her knees, I pull her body down on the couch so she was on her back; a knee positioned between her legs, I leaned over her, burying my fists in the cushions next to her head.

"You aren't stupid. Wanting your mother to give a shit about you isn't stupid. If anything she's stupid. She ruined a relationship with the smartest, funniest, most caring person I've ever met. Now, I don't know how much that means seeing as all I meet are spoilt assholes, but you get what I'm saying."

Tears were still slipping from her eyes, but she held a small smile on her lips.

"I'll take it, but you forgot to mention hottest."

"I thought it went without saying, my bad. She missed out on a great relationship, with the hottest person I've ever met."

She broke into a chuckle, making me grin in return. I lived for this feeling. Anytime I made her smile it felt like I'd achieved something beyond greatness.

I settled my arms by her side hugging her torso. Resting my head on her chest, I listen to her heartbeat through the fabric of her sweater as she ran her fingers through my hair and gently raked her other hand up and down my back. Her usual sweet cocoa butter scent was mixed with lavender, making me relax into her even more.

"Could you ever see yourself just up and running away, never looking back?" she spoke breaking the silence we sat in.

"I mean it depends, who am I running with and where are we headed?"

Her chest vibrated with another chuckle. My God, this girl. I was savouring everything about right now.

"What about Europe? You told me you used to toy with the idea of backpacking when you were younger. Why didn't you ever go with your best friend?"

"If this is your way of asking me to travel around Europe with you, I'm down. As far as the 'backpacking' part, my knees just told me not to fuck with them." She broke out into more laughter making me chuckle, but I wasn't playing.

"You just gonna skip over Ethan like that huh? .. I'm just wondering what it would feel like to get away for a while."

"First of all, Ethan is the only one calling himself my best-friend, and that's probably cause of all the ass it gets him. Secondly, if you need to get away for a little while, nothing is stopping us from leaving right now. Anywhere you want."

Taking us out of our bubble, the door opens and in strolls Sebastian. What the fuck?! I jump up grabbing my gun and aiming for his head. I shoot but he disappears. Turning back to Alesha, she's covered in blood holding a dead Sebastian in my place on her chest. She's looking back at me frightened as if I'm gonna hurt her, but she knows I would never lay an unloving finger on her. Right?

Before I can say anything, the sound of thunder jolts me awake. These dreams/nightmares are all I've been having lately. Real memories of me and Alesha plagued by that night.

I've tried giving her some space since everything happened, even I'll admit, it was a lot. Seeing that switch from happy, kinda turned on to 20% psychotic must've been a little jarring. I don't blame her though that 20% hit her at 100mph.

It's been 3 and a half weeks, she hasn't spoken to me and refused to answer her door. No matter how pissed I got, the last thing I wanted to do was scare her even more by breaking it down, but this separation thing's had a good enough run.

I even stopped myself from beating this dude's ass when I heard he'd taken her to fucking Paris and was staying an extra week after they were done working. Guys don't do that shit unless they're trying to fuck and I'm stopping myself from paying him a visit letting him know she's taken. I don't know if ya'll can tell, but I'm really trying to be the bigger person.

The ringing of my cell took me out of my thoughts. Seeing the caller ID, I answer already irritated by my train of thought. "What?"

"I see you're in your feelings. I was only calling to tell you that Dani and I are heading out so you won't be able to get hold of me until we land." Rafael replied.

"Fine. Remember I need you back here in 2 weeks tops. Where are you taking her anyway?"

"Uhhhm... well she wanted to go somewhere in Europe and she was talking about croissants and how she hasn't seen Alesha in a while and missed her so we're on our way to Paris."

He spoke so quickly I almost didn't catch any of what he said. Probably what he was trying to do.

"So you guys are planning to see... Paris?"

I could hear his sigh as he replied. "Yup we're gonna see.. Paris."

"I just remembered, I'm thinking about buying Grams a villa over there. What better way to house-hunt than in person? Get here in 30 minutes, we'll take the jet."

I hung up not waiting for a response. I packed a small bag of clothes and would be lying if I didn't say I was nervous and excited at the thought of seeing.. Paris again.

***

The whole flight Dani sent me smirks and gestures suggesting I had other intentions for joining them on this trip.

Raf spent his time on the jet whispering warnings about fucking up his and Dani's trip. The way he was freaking out you'd think he's got something major planned.

As soon as we landed, Dani's phone was pinging repeatedly with text notifications. The last one being the time and place Alesha wanted to meet for dinner.

We had just enough time to get to the hotel, take a shower and change. I did just so, making sure I was wearing the suit and cologne she loved most on me. I hadn't had the energy or time to cut my hair since.. well you know, so it was a little longer than usual. She always did want to see my hair grown out, I didn't hate it.

-

I was all nerves in the 15 minute drive to the restaurant. Raf could see how anxious I was and told Dani to go ahead.

"You've come this far you stubborn bastard, don't pussy out now. We got really lucky with those two and I'm glad you're fighting for her. Remember what Gramps used to say: 'it's not enough to be just enough for the people we love, we need to be greater'. Seeing you put in all this work for her- I'm just glad something finally means so much to you. I'm proud you're being greater, Chris."

He turns walking into the restaurant and I follow his lead. Stepping through the doors, my eyes scope out the room for her face.

There she is. Beautiful. My everything.

What the fuck is he doing here?

JJ x

Chapter 17 - Poor Dick Dunkirk

Alesha's eyes were trained on Christian as he walked further into the restaurant staring right back at her. Her focus dropped to the floor as Richard rest his hand on her lower back, leaning to whisper in her ear.

"If you want to leave just give me a sign."

She nodded her head sending Richard an appreciative smile.

Christian's blood boiled at how close this guy was to her. Trying to control his anger made his chest feel heavier.

"Dude take it easy. Don't make a scene." Rafael warned as they finally reached the table.

"Hey turtle boy. I've missed you." Raf grinned at the nickname as Alesha pulled him in for a hug.

"Sup, cognata."(Sister in law)

Christian smirked at Raf's reply. Alesha looked to Richard, who just shook his head as a sign to dismiss the comment. She turned back to the Marino brothers.

"Christian. It's good seeing you again."

His heart sulked a little at the stiffness of her greeting, but it started beating back to life when she laid her hands on his shoulders and leaned in for a kiss on his cheek. The smile stayed etched on his face as she pulled away.

He missed her. Her touches, her lips, her soothing voice that made the hair on the back of his neck stand up. He just missed her. All of her.

"You have no idea, il mio cuore."(My heart)

Alesha took a deep breath at the term and started blushing at the memories of when he used it most: when he was inside her making her toes curl and eyes roll to the back of her head.

Christian's smile widened at the fact he could still get her flustered.

"You haven't been introduced but I'm sure you both know of Richard."

Christian narrowed his eyes at Alesha while Raf reached out and shook the home wrecker's hand.

"Nice to put a face to the name. I've heard a lot of stories."

"All good I hope. Dani seems really happy, I'm glad she has someone looking out for her."

"They both have people willing to do anything for them." Raf spoke locking sights with Alesha.

Christian's attention flickered to the man stood in front of them with hand outstretched. 'How many limbs could I butcher before the shock killed him?' he wondered. 'Judging from experience, he looks like the type to pussy out at an arm and a leg.'

"Richard Dunkirk, pleasure to meet you."

"Christian Marino DeLuca. Nice to meet you too Dick." He addressed him with a seriousness, not even attempting to mask his malevolence with a civil smile.

"I prefer just Richard."

"That's nice."

Alesha shook her head at Christian's insolence. She could tell it was going to be a long night, and they hadn't even ordered the food yet.

-

"I remember it took me and 3 bouncers to hold you back. Only for you to break pass the barrier anyway. It's like I keep forgetting who you are, behind the fancy dresses and champagne flutes."

"Richard's right Dani, you know we're still banned from that club? Every time I pass by, the bouncers shake their heads."

"Y'all have got to take responsibility. Stop taking me to these places expecting me to act boujee. Can't none of you tell me you were good doing nothing while knowing Beyoncé was behind those curtains. Plus don't be all up on my ass when you both got autographs and a picture."

The whole table broke out in laughter while Dani side-eyed her friends.

"You all seem to be having a great time. Can I get you anything else?" asked the waitress who had been flirting with Christian the entire night.

"We actually spoke to the host a little earlier. He should have something prepared for us in the back." Alesha informed the waitress who still had all her focus on Christian.

"I'll get right on that. If there's anything else you need, just let me know." She smiled at him and he returned it as she walked away from the table.

Alesha felt a little pang in her chest at the fact he was entertaining the girl's advances. But she fought the feeling knowing she didn't have that right.

"So, tesoro, why are you in Paris?" Christian spoke directly to Alesha, after having enough of her avoidance all night, but she only returned an incredulous expression.(Sweetheart)

"Why are you asking when you already know?"

He smirked sitting back in his chair. She was talking to him, not scared or fearful of him. She seemed almost as annoyed as that time he forgot to pack her silk headscarf for their weekend away. Almost. He knew this conversation was most probably leading to an argument in front of their friends and Dick but he didn't care because she was finally talking to him.

"Is there something you want to say amore?"(Love)

"Two things actually:1. Stop with the pet names and 2. Tell Antoni, Ethan and the rest of your guys that if they're gonna follow me around all day everyday, a "hi" would be nice instead of lurking in the shadows."

Feeling the tension rise, Richard tapped her knee as a sign to calm down. Christian saw their silent conversation and could feel himself getting riled up.

"I won't apologise for keeping you safe. Perché stai provando a combattere con me? Stai cercando di farmi impazzire? Chiedi spazio e finisci a Parigi con questo stronzo?! Ne ho abbastanza di questa merda di "separazione"!

Enough!"(Why are you trying to fight with me? Are you trying to drive me crazy? Ask for space and end up in Paris with this asshole?! I've had enough of this "separation" shit!)

He leaned forward, dropping his fist on the table with the roar of his last command. Everyone sat motionless as his action caused the table's wine glasses and cutlery to clang against the dishes.

Alesha sent Christian a threatening glare as he stared back with his jaw clenched, emerald eyes burning into her deep hazel-toned ones.

After a few seconds of drowning out everyone else's looks while their gazes fought one another, Alesha turned to Richard. "Maybe we should call it a night. I think dinner's over."

Richard gave her a nod and stood, collecting their jackets from the backs of their chairs. At that moment the waitress came back over resting the decorated plate on the table.

"Happy 1 year anniversary you guys. It's from Richard and I. I'm sorry the meal had to end like this." Alesha kissed Dani and Raf's cheeks and headed to the exit. Richard pecked Dani's cheek and shook Rafael's hand. He even tried to shake Christian's but just followed Alesha when his gesture was ignored.

"Can we just get the bill?" Christian asked downing the last bit of his whiskey.

"That's already been taken care of courtesy of a.. Mr Dunkirk." The waitress said reading the receipt. "Is there something else I can get you. Something not on the menu?" She asked biting her bottom lip.

"Walk away. Now."

The waitress looked offended as her mouth gaped open. Christian paid no attention and just let out a deep sigh.

***

Back at the hotel Alesha was getting ready for a late night trip to the Eiffel Tower with Richard. He wanted to cheer her up a little after the dinner they'd just had and figured she'd like the peacefulness of the scenery.

Her hair was looking a little crazy. She was planning to take some pictures so tried using a straightener to add some waves but accidentally nicked herself with the iron. Needless to say she gave up and was opting for a bun instead. After holding an ice pack to it, the reddened mark was still a little sensitive.

She was still in her robe about to throw on some jeans and a sweater when there were knocks at her door. Richard told her to be ready in 45 minutes but it's only been 20. Why was he so early?

The knocks came again a little harsher this time.

"This boy playing around like we can't get kicked out the hotel." She mumbled to herself. "COMING!" She yelled as she ran from the bedroom. She pulled open the door as she tightened the silk strap of her robe. "I still have 25 minutes."

Looking up, her eyes widened as Christian stared back at her. Eyes raking over her body, he took a deep breath knowing she was naked underneath the thin fabric. Stepping into the room, he was immediately drawn to the small bruise on her neck.

He grabbed her chin turning her head to the side to get a better look. "What the fuck is this?"

She jerked her jaw from his grasp and stepped back. "Christian what are you doing here? I need you to leave."

The extra consumption of alcohol he had at the hotel lounge did nothing to help contain his aggravation. He was lucid, but his thoughts and behaviour were uninhibited. Not that he ever concealed the way he felt toward her anyway.

Stepping further into the room, he slammed the door and slowly stalked toward Alesha as she took steps back trying to keep distance between them. She cussed under her breath when she hit a wall.

"This is what we're doing now? All my days are spent stressing about how you're doing and figuring out how to make you forgive me, while you're jetting off to Paris and letting Dick fucking Dunkirk put his hands all over you?"

"I don't have to explain myself to you, but it's not like that. You should leave, we can have this conversation when you're not drunk."

"I'm not drunk. I just... ho bisogno di te."(I need you)

With barely any room between them, he leaned down closing his eyes and resting his forehead against hers. She could feel tears building behind her eyes at the sight of him being so broken.

"Richard isn't-"

"I just wanna know one thing, are you fucking him?"

JJx

Chapter 18 - My Heart, My Life, Everything

WARNING: MATURE SCENEREAD AT YOUR OWN DIS-CRETION

Christian

Pulling my head back, I opened my eyes seeing her lust-filled brown ones stare back at me. I loosened the knot of her robe's belt easing it off of her body to rest my hands on her bare waist.

A slight smile touched my lips when I saw the familiar contrast of my creamy white skin adorned in colourful tattoos, gliding against her rich cocoa tone which still felt smooth to the touch. I've missed this. I've missed her. It can't be possible to want someone this much.

I could feel my slacks tighten around my dick as I held her in my arms. "I'm only asking once more, il mio amore, are you fucking him?"

Infuriated by the thought alone, I felt my heart's rhythm speed up. I could hear my temper bleed through the tone of my question causing her to shiver under my hold.

"Christian it's not what you think it is, but at this point would you even believe me if I said no?"

She was right, the way they behaved around each other earlier kept my mind running wild with ideas of everything he could've been doing to her here while I was back home. But she's not that person, I know she isn't. She wouldn't sleep with some guy, especially not her boss, not after telling me she loves me. Not after seeing how determined I am to fix us; she still loves me. Doesn't she? She walked out, ..but that was out of fear, she was scared. My heart fought against my mind in an internal debate that did nothing but add fuel to my anger, and the alcohol did nothing to quell my jealousy.

Slowly winding my fist around her neck, I dipped to her ear, asking a question I knew would only set me off if given the wrong answer.

"Are you giving him my pussy Tesoro?"

I felt her breath quicken as she let out puffs of air against my collar. I could feel how fast her heart was beating from my finger resting on her pulse. I traced my hand along her side; feeling the silk skin of her curves under my fingers left me aching. My thumb skimmed across her hardened nipple as my fingertips travelled down her body. Finding my way between her legs, I slipped my finger past her wet lips to her swollen bud. I could feel the heat and slickness between her legs as she let out a soft, wispy moan. A sound that shook straight through me making my dick jump.

"Feels like you've missed me just as much." I removed my finger; looking into her eyes I put the soaking digit to my mouth and licked her essence. I could feel the thick pre-cum dripping from my cock. I stood back taking in her naked form in this moment as I confined her to the wall. She always looks so vulnerable under my gaze, so fucking beautiful.

I settled a kiss on her lips savoring their fullness and sweet taste. I thought I wanted her before, this was a whole new obsession. The excitement pulsated even harder through my erection when she teased my mouth with her tongue. I squeezed her neck tighter as I explored her mouth, pushing my bulge against her naked body, needing her to feel what she did to me.

Moving my hand from her throat, she watched as I hastily undressed, throwing my clothes to the ground. Gripping her sides, I picked her up, growing harder as she wrapped her legs around my waist.

I pushed her further into the wall leaving no space between it and our bodies. Reaching underneath her, I took a handful of my length and teased it against her entrance as I grazed her nipple with my teeth. Her moans vibrated in my ears. Looking into her glowing brown eyes, I locked my hand around her neck, pinning her to the wall.

Shoving my dick past her tightened walls, to the hilt of her, I breathed a trembling air of satisfaction and comfort as her pussy quivered around me. "Shit!"

A small whimper left her mouth as the wind was knocked out of her body. My grip on her throat kept her in place as I rammed into her over and over again. The slapping sounds our bodies made as they connected was drowned out by the loud cries Alesha couldn't suppress.

I pushed myself deeper into her, growing more and more desperate for her body with each moan she elicited. Her eyes began dimming as she came, her juices running down my shaft.

"You're mine, do you fucking hear me!" I gritted my teeth, speaking in a hushed growl. "Thought I would just let you go?"

The only things leaving her mouth were jumbled words and loud panting moans. I pulled out and ruthlessly rammed back into her over and over again, while her nails dug into my shoulders as she tried to grind against me. I let out a deep groan at the feel of her forcing herself down on my erection.

"Didn't I tell you this pussy, this body, you, belong to me?"

I let go of her neck grabbing her waist with both hands, slamming her down on my dick.

"CHRISTIAN!"

Within a few pumps her legs started shaking again as she hit her high. Her pussy was clenching around my dick so tightly there was no space to move. I walked her over to the couch and stood her up; her legs almost giving out before I caught her.

"Turn around and bend over." My tone was stern and final. She did just as I said, arching over the armrest of the chair, my cock was jumping, excited to enter her again.

I landed a few rough slaps on her ass and massaged the stinging skin, making her shudder. I rubbed the head of my dick against her wet slit before lining up with her wet pussy once again.

"Tu sei mio Alesha, lo sarai sempre."(You are mine Alesha, you always will be.)

Locking both her hands in my fist, I rest them on her lower back sliding into her. The warm narrow opening stifled my boner.

"Do you know what you mean to me? Sei il mio cuore ... la mia vita ... tutto."(You're my heart.. my life.. everything.)

I grunted my claims between each relentless stroke. Every time I pushed into her it was like her body was choking my cock, the feeling left me winded. I had to take a second; I didn't want to reach my end before I could release all the anger, jealousy and suffering I've been living under this last month.

She screamed through another orgasm as I kept thrusting into her tight cunt.

Pulling her up so her back was flush against my chest, I stuffed myself back into her; turning her face to me, I muffled her gasp with my lips.

Her head dropped to my shoulder and her eyes rolled back as I repeatedly sunk my cock deep inside of her, hammering against her walls.

I latched on to her lips hungrily, but when I reached around and massaged her clit with quick, intense rubs, she pulled away from my kisses allowing louder screams to escape. Her hand clasped my arm and I could feel she was about to reach another release.

Just as the sensation coursed through her, her pussy squeezed my dick, suffocating the throbbing erection. Losing the will to hold back anymore, I spurted rope after rope of my hot cum into her.

"If he's touched you, he's dead." I meant every word. Bypassing her short puffs for air, she pulled me in for a kiss, I could taste the desire for me on her tongue. She pulled away, ending it with a teasing bite on my bottom lip.

I can't do another day without this, without her.

JJ x

Chapter 19 - Elephant In the Room

Alesha

We lay there, hunched over the armrest of the sofa, for the longest time trying to catch our breath. My skin still tingled as dying shock-waves pulsed from between my legs. I could feel the warm air leaving him and beating against my back in between the kisses he trailed down my spine.

Three knocks rapped off of the hotel door. Immediately, my plans with Richard appeared in my head. I shot up as panic set in. "Babe, we've gotta get going. You better be ready." Richard's voice called from outside.

"Shit!" I murmured as I pushed myself off of the sofa and away from Christian, running to the bathroom. I peed then hopped in the shower trying to wash off the sweat as quickly as I could.

Once I got out, I threw on my jeans and sweater before clumsily running back to meet Richard at the front door.

"-she's busy."

Kill me now.

Christian stood in front of the open door butt-naked talking to Richard, who was examining the scene in front of him with widened eyes until his sights landed on me.

"Maybe I should leave you two to it?" Before I could say anything he walked away with a reddened face.

I stomped over to Christian pushing him back into the room and shutting the door.

"What the hell were you thinking?!" I felt my face heating up at the realization of what just happened. How do I even begin to apologize and explain what he just saw? Seeing the embarrassment and worry spread across my face, Christian decided to pipe up.

"What? You scared your little substitute is gonna get his feelings hurt knowing your man fucked you?" He smugly walked to the chair that I was bent over no less than 10 minutes ago. Grabbing a handful of the complementary candy from the coffee table, he took a seat.

I rolled my eyes at his impertinence, already frustrated with him. "Christian, please just get dressed and leave."

"No. I already told you, I'm sick of us being apart. I gave you your space and I'm ready to talk."

"Well what if I don't wanna talk? Ever." I didn't mean what I was saying, but I hated the idea of him being in control of when I was ready for things to change.

"Is that what you really want? You want me to leave you alone?"

Letting out an exasperated breath, I tilted my head to the ceiling, silently praying to God for more patience with this man. "Of course not. I just need you to respect me when I ask for a little time."

"A little time?! A, you've not spoken to me in a month. You won't let me in when I come to your apartment and you ignore my texts. That doesn't feel like you 'asking for a little time', it feels like you pushing me away."

He looked at me with hardened eyes, crushing my heart completely. Standing to pick up his clothes, he hauled on his boxers and slacks before sitting back down to stroppily shove his feet into his boots.

"Fine Chris, if you need to have this conversation right now, let's talk."

His eyes darted to me, wasting no time, he began firing off questions. "Do you want to end this?"

"No." I said truthfully.

"Then why do you need more space?"

"The night Dani called telling me about this 'mafia' stuff, a part of me panicked, but I ignored it because looking at you, I couldn't see a bad person, I only saw my best friend. What happened with Vasiliev- ...that night forced me to think about every side of you and what you do. I just need the space to decide if having you in my life is worth any more nights like that."

"Are you scared of me?"

"Chris, I was never scared of you. I just didn't know what you were fully capable of, and finding out gave me a lot to think about."

He nodded seemingly understanding where I was coming from. Looking down he propped his elbows on his knees, resting his head in his palms.

It went quiet for a while before he spoke, this time a little softer.

"Did you mean it; when you said you loved me?"

"Yes and I still do. With everything in me."

"Good. Perché anch'io ti amo, anche se so che ti meriti di meglio."(Because I love you too, even though I know you deserve better.)

I looked at him, confused by whatever he said; I could only make out an 'I love you'. Waiting patiently for his next question, another gust of silence passed. "...Are you fucking Dunkirk?"

"For God-sake, no!"

"Then why were you so scared for him to see us together?"

"He may be a close friend but he's still my boss. A boss you just exposed yourself to."

"So he's never tried anything with you?"

"He's married!"

"Doesn't stop some shitheads from trying."

"Put your shirt on and come with me."

I headed out the door leaving it open for Christian to trail behind. We walked down the hall and got the elevator up to the penthouse suite. I was feeling kind of nervous as I knocked and waited.

"What are we doing?" He had been confused since we left my room, but I continued to disregard his questions and comments.

Richard opened the door surprised to see us again.

I smiled slightly embarrassed thinking of earlier. "Hey, Christian just wanted to apologize for earlier and for dinner. But definitely for his.. display."

"I didn't say tha-" I nudged Chris in his side earning a death glare that I noticed in my peripheral. He stepped away from the entrance, leaning against the wall like a bored, frustrated child.

I shook my head showing Richard my irritation.

"Honey, is that room-service? I'm starving. Alesha? Hi sweetie. I'm so sorry I couldn't make it to dinner, I really wanted to meet those Marino boys, I hear they're drop dead gorgeous. Rich told me you had to cancel tonight because there was an elephant in your room." The remark was paired with a wink that made me cough on the air I breathed in, while Richard let out a chuckle.

"Darling, don't be crude." Richard smirked.

I turned to Chris, who had furrowed his brows in confusion at the additional voice. Pulling his arm to me, I brought him back in frame of the couple standing in the doorway.

"Christian Marino DeLuca meet Lucas Dunkirk, Richard's husband."

JJ x

Chapter 20 - Ultimatums

C hristian

"What took you so long?! We've only got 30 minutes before Dani gets here!"

I had just made it to Alesha's apartment after speeding through NY traffic during rush hour. As we made our way to her bedroom, I start stripping away my clothes; my dick already swelling at the sight of her in nothing but a short, silk, see-through robe.

"Why are we still hiding? We've been fucking since Paris, that's 2 weeks of running around behind everyone's backs instead of just saying we're back together."

"We've already talked about this, we aren't back together. Right now I'm stuck between wanting you in my life and not wanting to be a part of yours."

It felt like a ton of bricks just dropped on my chest. I clenched my jaw to avoid letting out a hurtful retort; sending her a narrowed stare, I stopped unzipping my jeans. She turned to face me with closed eyes letting out a deep sigh.

"You know that's not what I meant. I just need some time to get used to what you do. It's not like you leave the house everyday and go punch in a time card, Chris you kill people for a living. It's just not what I expected my future to look like, but please believe that I am trying."

I feel like shit when I see how the stress of the situation showed up on her features. Every time this conversation comes up I get angry. Not because I don't get it, but because I do and I think deep down she's already made her decision.

"It's been long enough, no? I mean you've had more than a month. I think you already know and you're just too scared to say it."

She slowly walked in my direction, only to stop right in front of me.

"Can we not fight right now? I just told you Dani's gonna be here in.." she looked down at the rose gold watch fastened around her wrist, "23 minutes. Please let's just be with each other and deal with everything else later?"

Her hands trailed from my chest to the waist of my jeans. The need to talk left me as I stared into her soft brown eyes looking back up at me. She reached her hand into my pants gently squeezing and stroking my hardening dick. My breathing hitched as she ran her thumb over my tip circling the pre cum around the head of my cock before retrieving her hand and sucking at her thumb.

The metal chimes of a key against the front door's lock stilled her movements. She scrambled to get me and my clothes out of view, but I couldn't move; I was too awestruck by what she just did, I didn't have the slightest interest in playing hide and seek.

"Bitch why the fuck do you have this door closed as if you didn't know I was coming?! Open up before I bust through this shit, I have something to tell you so stop playing these games with me!"

Dani screamed through the narrow opening of the door with the chain lock blocking her entrance.

"Christian! Why are you just standing there? You've gotta get out!" Alesha whisper shouted in a panicked tone. "COMING!" She yelled to Dani before turning back to me, "quick, use the fire escape."

I don't know what came over me, but I'd had enough and let my frustration get the better of me. "No! Right now, make the choice are you with me or not?"

She stopped moving, holding my jacket in one hand and one of my shoes in the other. Between the loud thumps Dani was applying to the door and the look Alesha was giving me, my head was about to explode. She was gonna give me an answer I didn't wanna hear.

"If I have to decide right now, then no." My stomach dropped at the response as she quickly blurted the rest of her answer. "But I'm trying to make it a yes, why can't you have the patience for that?"

"Because I'm not sure it's ever gonna be a yes. I know I put a lot on you when I introduced you to all this so I can't blame anyone but myself. You always play it safe A, so I know it's hard, but I'm asking you to trust when I say I won't let anything happen to you."

I could see the tears building in her eyes as she looked around the room avoiding my stare.

"It's not like I'm not trying Chris. Putting myself in a place where I'm depending on someone else for anything is new to me, especially when I'm looking to you for safety while people like Vasiliev are popping into our lives. You can't force me to hurry up and I can't force you to slow down."

"Alesha Ryan Moore! When I make it in this apartment I am gonna tear yo little ass up, best believe that!"

"So that's it?" The words burned at the skin of my throat as they came out.

"I don't want it to be, but Chris if you can't wait, then I guess so."

I grabbed my things from her hands and went to the door, where Dani seemed to have calmed a little after her threats. I unlocked the chain and was met with her grin as she held her hand up to my face.

"Rafael proposed!!" She paused realizing it was me answering the door. "You guys are back together?! Finally! And getting dirty in the middle of the afternoon, praise Jesus. I hope you forgive me for not telling you Richard was gay; jealousy breeds results. You're welcome."

"Congratulations Dani. I'll see you Sunday night."

I moved past her leaving a kiss on her temple. She turned her attention behind me, seeming confused by my rush to leave. As I made my way down the hall, I could hear Dani's voice doused in concern.

"What the hell happened?"

I turned in time to see her enveloping Alesha in a tight hug before walking into the apartment.

If a separation is what she wants, that's what she'll get. I'm done.

JJ x

Chapter 21 - Moving On & Passing Out

A lesha

Have you ever felt so disconnected from everything you become a sort of shell? A transcendent state where things are happening around you and your body is just reacting? Well that's been the past month for me.

He meant it. He wanted nothing to do with me anymore. There were no more calls, texts or unannounced visits to my apartment. With Vasiliev still around, he'd given Ethan and Antoni indefinite posts as my bodyguards. On the plus side, now that it wasn't a secret, they insisted on driving me everywhere. Having 3 buff guys ready to follow and drive me anywhere, that was a whole mood for your girl.

We were on our way back to my apartment after capping off a list of errands I had to do after work.

"You still nervous about meeting Rochelle's dad?" I looked over to Antoni who was sitting next to me, his head popped up from his phone.

"Are you kidding? It means so much to her for him to like me; I just hope I don't fuck this up."

"Maybe you guys can bond over the whole ex-navy seal thing. Just pray to God her sisters don't show up, from what she's told me they're both a piece of work."

"It's cool, she's been soaking our place in holy water, they'll probably burn trying to cross the threshold." The whole car started laughing, even Dom wore a slight smirk.

At 6'7" and 327lbs of muscle, Dominic was easily an intimidating guy for anyone who didn't really know him. Even some of the made-men that worked for Christian, tended to avoid him. I couldn't blame them, I've never seen his sweet, calming and kind demeanor shown to anyone else except me and Dani, but it was comforting knowing it was there. He was a faint reminder of my dad in a way, so since meeting him I preferred having him around.

The hard, emotionless side of him was one I understood and never questioned after hearing how the guys came to nickname him, 'Dome', which I hated.

While he was out with some friends, a crazed ex boyfriend murdered his wife in cold blood.. in their bed. The other man had been obsessed with Dom's wife, Maya, since she left him a few weeks before meeting the sweet giant.

Dom unwittingly got home that night only to catch the psycho in the act. The man launched at him, explaining the poorly healed scar that ran across his face, from his hairline to the top of his lip. They spared me the details on how Dom dealt with him, but told me how he'd suffered a mental breakdown after. Taking pleasure in scalping his victims as torture; when he caught them, his first incision was a clean one around the person's head and from there, between abuses ranging from whippings and electrocutions all the way to dissections, he would pull back their scalp inch by inch, listening to their screams.

They said he was much better now, but I still felt for the poor man. Whenever he was around I tried to make sure the vibe was light and fun, hopefully getting him out of his head for a while. It seems stupid but it worked most times, I've seen him crack his fair share of smiles when he couldn't hold back.

The car drifted back into the habitual chitchat until I asked the usual question that played on my mind. I know the guys were probably bored of the everyday debrief but I needed to get my fill.

"So.. how's he doing?"

Antoni and Ethan turned their head in the direction of the window closest to them, while Dom kept his eyes glued to the road. The silence was covered by sporadic coughs and humming.

"What aren't you guys saying?"

"A, maybe you should go see him, then you'll get your answer." Ethan turned to me, his voice was sympathetic but his eyes seemed guilty.

".. Is he still with her?"

Again, everyone's eyes avoided mine.

"I'll take that as a yes. Listen, you guys don't need to feel weird about it. He's moved on, so should I. If he's happy then I'm happy for him."

"Non so se è quello che chiamerei "felice"." Antoni murmured under his breath, getting a look from Ethan.(I don't know if that's what I'd call "happy")

I hated when they spoke Italian. I could only pick up on certain words that Chris had taught me, so I was lost in conversation most of the time. Richard had tried teaching me too, but there was no use; different languages were never my speciality, I was still trying to master English.

The car pulled up to the curb and Antoni got out holding the door open for me. As soon as the smell of the vendor's hotdogs hit me, I felt my stomach churn. Running to the closest garbage can, I threw up my lunch. Thankfully, Ethan was behind me pulling my hair from my face and patting my back; I was about to be pissed because I had only just had wash day yesterday.

My stomach settled after a few minutes, but as I stood straight my entire body felt weak and dizzy. Noticing my unbalanced frame, Dom picked me up bridal style. I must've been more worn out than I thought because all I remember was resting my eyes and drowning everyone out.

JJ x

Chapter 22 - It's Stacey, Asshole

- -

C hristian

I lay back on the couch while she took off her sweater, but as always, nothing she did excited me.

Stella has a cute face and a body most guys would love to have draped across their laps, but I felt nothing. A month now and I've only been able to get off by picturing Alesha whenever she touched me or I touched myself.

This had gotten way out of hand. Seeing me 'move on' was supposed to make her realize what we had was what she wanted, but I should've known better. She wasn't like the girls I normally fucked with, she didn't throw tantrums and come running back when I pushed her away. She did the one thing I didn't want her to do.. listen.

Seeing me with Sophie only nudged her towards the single life and me to every bottle in reach. Maybe she just wasn't as into me as I thought.

.. Fuck that. She loves me whether she wants to or not. I know it, she knows it and her body tells me every fucking time I touch her.

I was slightly relieved at the sound of my ringtone when Sabrina lowered her head attempting to put her lips to mine. The abrupt reach for my phone left her lunging, face first into the back seat of the couch.

"Hello?"

"Hey. How soon can you get down to St Anne's?"

"What are you doing at the hospital E? If this is another one of your sexual adventures gone wrong, call somebody else. I'm not about to sit in a waiting room for half a day because your toy of the week wanted to try something new."

"In the 20 years I've known you that only happened twice and I learn from my mistakes. We're here for A, sh-"

I stood too fast, knocking Stephanie off my lap and to the floor. Too engrossed in the news coming from the other side of the line, I leave her there, making my way to the front door. "What happened? Is she okay? Is she hurt? In pain? Where were you and-"

"She emptied her guts in a trashcan and then passed out so we brought her here. She's asleep now, but after the doctor came to see her, she asked for you."

Putting on my shoes and pulling my jacket off the hook, his words surprise me a little. "Wait.. she actually asked for me?"

"Yeah but- man just get down here as soon as you can."

"I'll be there in 15." Hanging up, I open my door to leave but remember I have company. "Hey Sarah! I've got somewhere to be, come on let's go!"

She came running out of the living room, wrestling to get her sweater back on, wearing an annoyed expression. The only thing I felt bad about was the fact that I didn't feel bad; the longer she took getting out, the longer it was before I could see A.

"It's Stacey, asshole. Almost a month making love to me and you still refuse to learn my name. I bet Moore wasn't doing half the shit I do to you and definitely not as good."

There was no hesitation after those words left her mouth, I wrapped my hand around her throat lifting her off the ground and squeezing hard enough to put her in pain but not enough to kill her, sadly. I sent her an unbothered expression as she scratched at my hand while I felt her larynx bobbing against my palm.

"We were fucking. That's it. You think I saw you behind that front desk and fell in love or some shit? I don't need to know your name Sally, you were placeholder pussy and couldn't even get that right. You don't talk about her, ever. If she sees you around that office you don't say shit to her unless you're spoken to; you so much as say her name after today and I will kill you. Understood?"

She continued scraping at my arm, legs kicking at my shins and eyes drooping closed. Rolling my eyes in boredom I let her go; dropping to the floor and clutching her throat, she gasped at the air trying to catch her breath. So melodramatic. I would've stopped if she passed out. Probably. I would've probably stopped if she passed out. Removing my gun from its holster, I knelt down and used the barrel to raise her chin so we were face to face.

"Now, I've never had a problem putting women in the red and I'm telling you now, that's not a nice place to be. Sydney, you seem real.. simple; so, I'll give you another chance to give me the right answer. You will take everything I've said and put it into play. Am I understood?"

She let out a raspy "yes" nodding her head, tears slid down her reddened cheeks and her eyes bulged from their sockets trained on the gun lifting her sore throat. At this point I feel I'd be doing her, and everyone who knows her, a favour by pulling the trigger, but I decide against it knowing she's already made me later than I wanted to be.

"The woman I actually want is in a hospital waiting for me and you just wasted a whole bunch of my time so we really should be on our way." She stood still, staring in shock. The irritation in my voice was clear as I spoke louder, scaring her even more, "get the fuck up and out Sadie!"

She scrambled to her feet running out of the house with her shoes in hand. Closing the door I wondered why she was still stood in front of my jeep with eyes stuck to the pavement. I got in the car and remembered I drove her here and there was no bus service in or near my neighbourhood. Hitting my head against the steering wheel I rolled the window down.

"I really don't have all day just get in the fucking car."

***

Alesha

I woke up in the hospital bed with Dani by my side skipping through the channels on the small tv, Winnie asleep in a chair to my left, Ethan babbling in quiet whispers on the phone and Dominic posted in a dark corner of the room.

"Look who's awake. You scared the hell outta me little girl." Dani teased, grabbing my hand with a big grin on her face.

My head was pounding to the point I could hear my heart beating in my ears.

"Have they told you?" I asked Dani motioning to the two men in the room.

She shook her head no, "Ms. Winnie told the doctor she was your grandma, so they let her know before I got here."

"I was really hoping the whole conversation was a dream. What do I do now? Dani, you know I can't do this, right?" I had slowly started freaking out. Close to an anxiety attack, I tried controlling my breathing but my hearts beat just kept getting harder to keep up with. The beeping of the machine started getting louder and faster, mimicking my current panic which didn't help either.

"Lee, look at me." I looked to her, copying the deep breaths until I felt steady again. "You'll be okay. We'll handle it the same way we do everything else: together. I've got you, always, but you have to tell him."

"I know, I know. I've already asked Ethan to give him a call."

"He'll help, Lee. As much as you try to ignore it, you know he'll do anything for you. Even if you can't be with him yet, at least trust that man's love for you. He's obsessed."

I simper at the comment knowing she wasn't far from the truth. I squeezed her hand tighter hoping that doing so would take away my worries and fears, but my best friend could only do so much to ease my mind. "It's not so much him I'm worried about. What if she's right?"

"She's not part of our lives anymore, are you really gonna let her stop you from being happy? Genuinely happy? It doesn't matter what she said, you and I both know that woman is full of Grade A bullshit. You've done more than enough to prove you're nothing like her." Dani sat back in her chair looking at me with narrowed eyes, as if trying to find something in my eyes.

Tell me something, did you push away from him because you were scared you guys would actually make it? I know the whole Vasiliev thing was a lot for you, but that's not why you left is it? You believe her. Every single word she said, you believe it, and that's why you don't want him."

I love my best friend, more than life sometimes, but there are times when I would like my thoughts to stay in my head and my head alone. "You know, after that day, I was paranoid for the longest time thinking you would leave like she said and it would be just me and her; like I'd never be able to get away. Yet every single day I got up, you were waiting for me outside in that busted old car." I let out a chuckle remembering how she loved that death-trap. A second of silence passed as I tried to fight the tears threatening to pour from the corners of my eyes. "Did you bring any food? I'm starving and I refuse to eat any of this hospital crap."

I looked in Winnie's direction avoiding the sympathetic look Dani was giving me. "I'll always be here for you, but that's not an answer." I could feel her brush my hair behind my ear, a move she always did when she wanted to play Oprah and have me bawling.

"Stop it Dani. I'm fine. I'll be fine."

All of a sudden the door burst open making Dominic lift his gun and Winnie jump from her sleep. Christian took in everyone who occupied the small space before his eyes landed on me.

"Can you guys give us a minute please?" I asked holding his stare with my own.

Dani and Winnie squeezed my arm while the boys sent me small nods before they all ushered out of the room. He moved slowly toward me taking in our surrounding. His eyes darting from my face to the heart monitor, which filled the silence with that incessant beeping, then to the needle in my arm.

Finally settling for a seat at the foot of my bed he rubbed my legs over the sheets, wearing a cocky smirk. "You didn't need to do all this to see me, you could've just called, I would've answered."

"I'm 6 weeks pregnant." His movement stopped and his smirk grew into an ear to ear grin.

"We're pregnant?!"

"No no no no. I'm pregnant, you participated." I teased.

"You were bound to have my baby, the way we go at it. I'm just surprised it took so long." His grin dimmed as he moved his hand up to rub my stomach "you have no idea what this means to me A."

"I do."

"What does this mean for us? You already know where I stand with every-thing. I don't want to raise this baby as a single dad; I need you in both our lives." I couldn't help but smile at the glint of hope in his eyes.

"Raising a kid isn't something I ever thought I'd do, and it definitely isn't something I ever want to do without you. Maybe we can give us anoth-"

The door flew open again and in strode Stacey with her ever evident bitchiness.

He brought her here? Was he expecting me to declare some undying love for him while she sat in the waiting room?

Ignoring my presence completely she turned to Christian. "I have work tomorrow, are you ready to go?"

The anger was clear in his eyes, I could see the redness rising from his neck as he got off of the bed stepping closer to her. "What the fuck do you think you're doing?" He stood in front of her and whispered something else before she took off running from the room scared with tears in her eyes.

"You're still with Stacey."

"I was never with Stacey." I deadpanned, giving him an 'are you serious' look. "You know what I mean. I was never with Stacey like that, like I was with you, like I want to be with you."

"Her being here, being a part of your life, that wasn't you wanting to be with me. That was you trying to hurt me." I rubbed my sore eyes holding in my tears. "With where we're at right now, it's probably best we try co parenting fir-"

"Fuck that, not happening. Yes, I was being childish and petty, I'll admit it, but that's because I don't know what it takes to get through to you. For months I have been trying to get you back and everything I do doesn't seem to be enough. I need you in my life and now you're having our kid, how much clearer does it need to get for you?"

"There was never an issue of your efforts being good enough. You know why I asked for my space Chr-"

"FUCK YOUR SPACE!"

He bellowed from the top of his lungs, pushing the food tray that stood at the end of my bed, to the ground. We stared each other down again until Winnie came back into the room, putting a hand on Christian's chest to soothe him.

"Sweetheart, go take a walk and calm down a little. You both could do with some space right now."

"Will everyone please stop saying that shit! Space is the last thing I need; that's what started all this fucking bullshit in the first place! I love you, that should be enough! Do you not want me, is that it? You want someone better? Somebody who actually deserves you? You wanna spend your life fucking someone because he's safe?!" He kept his eyes locked on me, aiming every word like a knife at my chest.

"Christian! Go home, get some rest and think about how it is you want to behave toward the mother of your child."

He broke his gaze from me, looking to Winnie and then back to me once more before walking out the door and slamming it behind him.

"He's never acted like that before. I'm sorry sweetheart, he just needs some time to cool off. I'll send Dani back in and go get you girls something to eat." Winnie offered looking at the food spilt over the floor, before leaving me alone with my thoughts.

I couldn't help the flood of all the pent up tears trickling down my face. What the fuck is my life right now?

JJ x

Chapter 23 - Ms Esther

Danielle

The brightly lit hospital room was a stark contrast to the mood right now. It was dark outside meaning visiting hours are probably over soon. My sister was still laid up in this uncomfortable ass looking bed, exhausted from all the crying she'd been doing since Chris stormed out of here. I love this girl with all my heart but she is so stubborn sometimes. I know she had her reasons to be, but damn. It hurts having someone you care about go through so much and not be able to fix it all for them.

I agreed with Chris that she had to give him a fair shot but I will cut my own arm off and eat it before I publicly side with someone else over my best friend.

If only he put his man-whore ways aside and actually dealt with her patiently like an adult by giving her the time she needed. I think I did enough scolding and cussing after we found out he was sleeping with the receptionist from her office. Yes, that hurt her, but I know for a fact that the trifling heifer has nothing to do with Alesha rejecting him again.

She's scared. Of course she's scared. I'd be worried if she wasn't. I knew our past would fuck her up. How could it not? But it's been years, why let it affect us now when we're enjoying life? She deserved to be happy, she deserved to have someone put her first, she deserved him.

"Did you let him leave because you really don't think you two would work out? Or did the idea of letting him in scare the shit outta you?" I kept my voice levelled not wanting the words to come out harsh or heartless. My attention stuck on her puffy, red eyes waiting for a reply.

"Dani, I don't feel like doing this right now. I've got a lot to figure out. Please just- not right now." She laid her head back on the padded white pillows, staring up at the ceiling.

She sounded so lifeless and her eyes were so dull and emotionless, I was instantly reminded of the girl 9 years ago wh-

"I never wanted all this. For the first time in my life I was feeling free and normal like I didn't have all that baggage following me around."

Her words broke my heart. I scooted my chair as close to the bed as I could, holding her hand in mine. "It wouldn't be baggage if you told him and got it off your chest. I'll never know why you see all of what you went through as a weakness. Do you know how strong you are? How fucking amazing? For someone to experience everything you have and make it out the other side like you did? These people want us in their lives Lee. Don't push them away."

When I felt the warm droplets hit my chest, I wiped away the tears I didn't know were falling from my eyes.

"Have you told Rafael everything?" She turned her head to the side looking back to me.

"I'm marrying him for Christ sake. Of course I've told him about his fucked up future in-laws." That got her to let out a small chuckle. "I didn't tell him about you though, I figured it wasn't my place."

"It's as much your past as it is mine. You had to go through it as well, you have as much right as I do." She turned her sights back to the ceiling.

The older nurse that had been checking in on us throughout the day walked in with a fresh bag of saline to swap out the drip. "Evening ladies. I'm sorry honey, but visiting hours ended a few minutes ago." I sent her a playful pout. "It's just an overnight stay, mom-to-be gets discharged tomorrow morning."

"Okay." I leaned down to kiss A all over her face like she was a toddler, which made her laugh as she hugged my neck.

"I love you."

"I love you too, boo." She squeezed me a little tighter not wanting to let go. "Stop thinking everyone is gonna leave if you let them in. I'm still here." I kissed her cheek once more before easing off of her. I stood up and brushed her hair from her face before straightening my shirt. "I'll be back tomorrow morning to pick you up. Don't cause Nurse Patricia any trouble." I said pointing to the smiling nurse.

I waved to them, exiting the room. Dominic and Antoni stood outside on each side of the door monitoring whoever came and left, which put my mind at ease knowing that Vasiliev guy was still roaming free.

"Danielle, I'm supposed to take you home. You ready?" Ethan asked walking from the nurses station, where he was more than likely hitting on the poor women.

"I'm ready, but there's a little pit stop I wanna make."

***

Walking up the steps to the mansion, I feel a little nervous at what I was about to do, but it would be for the best in the end. I knocked on the door and was greeted by Gio, one of the many men Christian had posted around his house. "Hi, is he here?"

"Yes ma'am, in his office."

Passing the boy who was no less than 18 years old, I made my way through the house to see Chris. Getting to his office I knocked and walked in. He was sat behind his desk, head falling over the back of the chair with his feet crossed at the ankles and propped up on the expensive wooden table, which took me forever to find and restore, but whatever. His head shot up as I took a step inside the office. Realizing it was just me, he raised his glass emptying the contents.

"I need to talk to you."

"I don't think I'm in the mood to be talked to, Dani."

"Too bad." I moved closer to him, taking a seat at one of the chairs in front of his desk.

"What is this? She get you to come set me rules or something?"

I let out a sigh as the room fell silent. Taking a deep breath, I made the final decision that this was the right thing to do. If I don't, she will keep self sabotaging. Plus, it's my past too, right?

"I know you don't know much about her history except that she doesn't like talking about it, but do you know why she never wanted a family? Like, no husband, no kids?"

He dropped his feet from the desk, leaning forward with a grimace. "She's not aborting my baby."

"Chris, no! For God sakes." His face relaxed as I took another breath before starting again.

"Everyone knew Ms Esther and Papa Damon loved each other like crazy, but when he died nobody could've expected Ms Esther to react the way she did. She fell into this depression unlike anything I've ever seen before. You could talk to her til the cows came home and she wouldn't say a thing back. We had this horrible storm one week straight and she spent that whole week sat outside on the porch in one of the rocking chairs he made, just a blanket draped across her shoulders. Alesha and I tried convincing her to go inside but each time we tried you would think she was a wild animal the way she swung at us. We brought her food and water but she wouldn't eat, wouldn't talk, just sat there looking out into the fields. Some folks said she was either waiting for Papa Damon to come back or she was trying to join him.

Eventually, CPS came around and told her that if she wanted to keep Alesha she would have to prove she could be a fit parent. Ms Esther knew she couldn't lose Lee as well, so she did what she thought would help. She tried drinking to forget, but that only made her violent. I managed to get away with a couple minor scratches, but Lee has her fair share of scars from those months. Since that first visit, Lee did what she could to hide Ms Esther's real shit from CPS, scared where she'd end up if they took her away.

One day we got home and I could never forget Alesha's face. In the 3 years since losing her dad, that was the happiest I'd seen her. She thought her mom was better, the woman was bouncing off the walls, had made enough cookies to feed the whole town and was talking so fast it all sounded like one long mumble session. But she seemed happier and that made Alesha happy, so I rocked with it. Turns out the local dealer came to the house a little while after, saying Ms Esther owed him money. She'd started taking coke thinking it could do a better job than the liquor. Alesha had to sell the locket her dad gave her for her last birthday with him, just to pay that piece of shit back.

Anyway, it must've all gotten to be too much and the next day I went to pick her up for school, I found her.. and there was so much blood.. had I gotten there a minute later- I don't know. After the paramedics came and loaded her into the ambulance, Ms Esther came stumbling out of her bedroom with the same prick that had taken the most important thing from her daughter. I didn't say anything, just got in my car and followed the EMTs to the hospital. The whole drive there and the week following, I blamed myself for not being able to see all the signs that led my best friend to that place, but that blame quickly honed in on her mom. When she finally made her way to the hospital, instead of being thankful her daughter was still alive, she started spouting a whole bunch of bull. I could never forget her words if I wanted to.

"You think I haven't tried? You know what, it's a damn shame Danielle found you, you would've been better off with your father. This was never a family, it was a mistake, and you'll feel the exact same if you ever have a man promise you the world only to leave you stranded with a kid you never wanted. Never did me any good and look at where you are now, destined to end up like dear old mommy. I'm telling you this cause you're my child, my blood: 'families' aren't for people like us, we live to see the ones we love either die or abandon us, so don't get too attached. That's the best advice you'll ever get from me."

I have never cussed out one of my elders like I did that woman. To say all that to her 15 year old daughter who just tried to take her own life? What makes it worse, I think she believes her. It was a lot to hear from the woman who raised her, who was supposed to be on her side, who actually was up until the day Papa Damon died. The way she treated Lee those 6 years, the things she said to her, I've only imagined how much worse it was when I wasn't around. My parents were money-hungry demons who didn't give a shit about me, but they never went out of their way to tear me down like that. You might think she's fighting against you so hard because you don't deserve her, but it's probably because she doesn't think she deserves you. Chris, all I'm saying is, some people need to be fought for a little harder than most."

***

Christian

I was standing at the foot of Alesha's hospital bed admiring how beautiful she was as she slept, mouth slanted open and all; she looked so peaceful and calm.

Walking to the other side of the room, I kicked off my shoes and got under the covers. Wrapping my arm around her waist, I pulled her into me, burying my face into her soft curls that smelt of pineapples and coconut.

Picking up her hand I looked at her wrist trying to find any semblance of a scar. It was faint but it was there. The back of my eyes burned remembering all of what Dani told me. I pulled her even closer to me, but close didn't feel close enough, until she wrapped her arm around mine, resting it on her stomach.

"I'm sorry." Her voice was soft and raspy making my skin heat up.

"Baby, I'm the one who's sorry. For everything. You have no idea how much I've missed you."

"I can't be your baby now that we're actually having one."

"What are you talking about? I can have more than one baby, in fact I can't wait to start working on number 3."

"We're not even halfway with this one."

"Practice makes perfect. ..How do you feel, really? Are you okay?"

"I'm trying to be."

"There is no one I would rather have be the mother to my children. No one I know who could do a better job. No one more worthy of my love and respect."

"Not even that lady we saw at lunch wearing the hot pink fishnets, silver booty shorts, that 'just livin' crop top and 8 inch stripper heels? You two would make some interesting kids."

"I almost forgot about her." I said motioning to get out of the bed before laughing at Alesha pulling me back down. I settled back into my spot, still chuckling. "Not even her. I mean it... I'm here as long as you'll have me, which better be forever."

JJ x

Chapter 24 - Okay, Perfect

{ Friday 4am}

Alesha

"I swear I would've gone myself, but when I tried getting up the nausea had me spinning." He only woke up once he felt the bed and realized I wasn't next to him. Coming back from the bathroom, I managed to make it to one of the chairs before I could pass out on the bedroom floor, but I didn't want to worry him, he stresses over me and peanut way too easily.

Chris stood at the foot of the bed pulling on his jeans. "Are you kidding? I wouldn't have let you go anywhere by yourself, especially this time of night. Besides, these spontaneous food runs make me feel like you actually need me through this pregnancy."

"I'll always need you.. to get me food." I said taunting him, he let out a laugh shaking his head. "Seriously though, I know I'm driving you crazy, but I haven't slept more than 6 hours over the last 4 days and the only thing my body wants right now is that spicy deluxe sandwich, a strawberry lemonade and about 20 of those chicken nuggets. Or to throw up. Oh, and some chocolate for later too."

He laughed harder as he sat down to put his shoes on. "I will get you your chocolate, and as for sleep, is it the bump that's uncomfortable or are you still having those dreams?"

"Those are too real to be dreams, I'm telling you something doesn't feel right." I raised a brow, with a skeptical tilt of my head. "If you're not letting me come are you sure we can't ask one of the guys to go instead? Or you could just make me a bacon sandwich, and no-one has to leave the house."

He stood up picking up his hoodie and walked over to me. Pulling me up from the chair he placed a tender kiss on my lips, drawing back to look into my eyes. "You asked for it and I'm gonna get it for you. I'll be fine. We've talked about this, it's probably just mama bear nerves, I'll be okay." I gave him a look that let him know I was against this. He walked me over to the bed, turning me around for another peck. "We will be okay and our son will be perfect. If it makes you feel any better I'll take one of the guys with me."

"I don't know-" He leaned in for another kiss. I pulled him closer to me deepening it, loving how his lips moved against mine.

"If you want that food I'm gonna need you to let me go before I'm the one eating some chocolate." I couldn't hold back my laugh as he playfully squeezed my ass. He helped me into the bed, kissing me once more before pulling away and heading for the door. "I love you."

"I love you too. Don't forget the chocolate!"

"I'd rather die."

"Stop playing with me." I could hear his chuckles from the hall as I put my head down to relax.

-

{Friday 4pm}

I woke up feeling the most rested I've felt since being pregnant. Looking around the room, I notice that I'm alone and Christian's side of the bed is as cold and empty as he left it this morning. Reaching for my phone I tried calling him but was sent straight to voicemail. Trying another 4 times, I'm sent to the same robotic voice. Hoping he's downstairs waiting for my lazy ass, I get up and make my way to the kitchen.

Antoni was sat at the breakfast bar, eyes glued to his phone as usual.

"Hey Toni, have you seen Chris?"

He looked up, seemingly confused by the question. "Hey. Uhh, no I haven't. I got the food for you like he asked, but by the time I got back here you were fast asleep. So if you want, there's a couple cold nuggets and a half a bar of chocolate in the fridge." I just stood there, staring at him in disbelief. "What? I was hungry and those things don't taste that great reheated. I did you a favor." He dropped his head bringing his attention back to the cellphone in his hand. No he didn't.

I picked up an apple from the fruit basket, throwing it at his head. "Next time, eat that; hot or cold, I want my nuggets." I turned to the pantry to grab a bag of chips and then got my chocolate and a water from the fridge. "So he didn't go with you? Did he say where he was going?"

"Nope. He left with Dome and called me about an hour later asking me to pick up all this junk food, but that was a little after 5 in the morning; I haven't spoken to him since. You might wanna get dressed, we have to leave for the engagement party soon and you take forever."

"You are really trying me today, huh. Eat my food and now you putting me on the clock?" I could hear him chuckling as I left the kitchen and headed back upstairs.

-

As soon as I was done getting dressed I tried calling Christian again, but still no answer. I didn't want to show it, but the fact that no one had heard from him or Dominic since this morning made me a little uneasy. I pushed the feeling aside and made my way back downstairs to see Antoni already at the front door. "You look beautiful. Ready to head out?"

"As ready as I can be with a 2lb bowling ball sitting on my bladder. Still no word from him?"

"None. Try not to worry, Raf probably just needed some help making everything perfect for Dani tonight."

I nodded my head convincing myself he was right and my anxiety was pregnancy prone. "Maybe he needed a little break. He's been waiting on me hand and foot for the past 5 months. That's enough cravings, exhaustion and mood swings to bring any grown man to his knees."

"Are you kidding, he lives for that stuff. You say jump and he asks how high with a shit-eating grin on his face. There is no world where he would willingly take a break from you."

***

We got to the restaurant where the line of cars waiting for valet was endless.

Antoni looked ahead at the countless row of cars and let out a groan. "Did Dani invite all of New York to this thing? We should've asked Berto to drive. We'll be stuck here all night, probably better off finding our own parking."

Once we managed to finally leave the car and get into the event hall, we were instantly stunned by the lavishness that should've been expected. This was Danielle Taylor's party after all.

Dani immediately spotted us and made her way over, tugging a smitten Rafael alongside her. "Hey girl. I'm so glad you're finally here. I was starting to forget how and why I know some of these people."

"I told you not to be tipsy every time you meet someone new, you'll end up thinking everybody's cute and funny. Are you guys enjoying yourselves so far?"

"It's been good. I'm just ready to get her the fuck out of here and back home. I got her so close to cancelling a couple hours ago when I was hitting it like my life depended on it." He looked over to Dani biting his bottom lip as his eyes trailed from her chest to her face. Antoni's face swiftly mimicked my own disgusted one.

"We would like to get as far away from all this as possible, so could you please point me in the direction of my man?"

"Chris didn't come with you?" Rafael tore his eyes from Dani to give me a deadpan stare. His always playful face had a serious expression which had me thinking the worst.

"No. We haven't heard from him all day. That's what I tried calling to talk about. I figured you guys were just too busy setting up. Have you not seen or heard from him?"

"Not since last night. Don't worry, he probably got side tracked baby proofing something you won't need."

"I don't know. I've had the weirdest feeling lately. I swear to God when I find this man I'm gonna kill him for making me worry like this."

"Who you gonna kill?" I spun around at the familiar voice that made my heart race in relief.

"Where the fuck have you been?!" I whisper shouted slapping his arm. "Do you know how long I've been calling you?! What was so important that it took you all day and put me on the verge of hourly panic attacks?"

"I will tell you everything later, I promise. But for now I'd like a kiss from my girl. I've missed you." He leaned in for a kiss and I turned my head still slightly annoyed at his disappearance. "Baby, don't be like that. I swear I'll make it up to you the minute we get home." His words whispered in my ear, forming goosebumps on my arms.

"You better put in some work."

"When have I never?"

"Okay, it's clear you couples don't give a shit who hears what, so I'm gonna make my way over to the bar and try to drink away everything I just heard." Christian's kisses drifted from my ear to my neck as Antoni walked away.

After getting back together, it's like everything I felt for this man intensified. Every kiss and touch made me ache for more of him. I hung to every word and sound of laughter he uttered. I was even in awe of how handsome he was; the way his face would scrunch in concentration or how his laugh made those green eyes light up. But the one thing I couldn't fall any more deeper in love with was the entirety of how much he loved me.

-

Tonight felt easy, it felt simple and this is exactly what I wanted the rest of my life to feel like. I sat back relaxing in my chair as Christian draped his arm over my shoulder while he brainstormed couples getaways with Richard and Lucas. He looked peaceful and genuinely happy, I loved seeing him this way, no stress, no worries, just enjoying himself.

Wait. Why is he this happy? Since Vasiliev, there's not been a second that's passed where he hasn't scoped out his surroundings. Even with the security guards he hired, he would still constantly check the exit and entry points as well as the faces of every single person in the same room as us.

"You found him, didn't you?" I cut in on their conversation.

He turned his head to meet my eyes. "What are you talking about?"

"That's why you're in such a good mood, you found him."

He winked at me with a small smile before turning back to Richard. I immediately relaxed against his arm, resting my head on his shoulder and the odd feeling I've had all day washed away instantaneously. He was right, we're okay and our baby is perfect.

The party didn't have to go on for much longer before the fatigue stopped me in my tracks. We said our congrats and good nights to the happy couple, leaving the lively party. Antoni went to pull the car around while I snuggled into Christian's warm chest, breathing him in.

He lifted my chin to meet his gaze. "You better get all your rest in the car because that pussy is mine when we get home." Planting a breathtaking kiss on my lips he pulled away when someone tapped his shoulder.

"You're Christian Marino."

"And who are you?"

Before either of us could register what was about to happen the man raised an iron clad fist knocking Christian to the ground. Within the time that my eyes had shifted from the blood seeping out of Christian's head to pay attention to the face stood in front of me; the man's hand had plunged toward my stomach. Retracting his fist he repeated the motion over and over again with quick strikes, leaving a piercing pain in my side. My body tensed at the menacing grin on his face.

"Julian Howard sends his condolences."

Just as fast, Christian was back up and charging for him. Without hesitation, Chris tackled him to the ground throwing rough punches at the man. His fists struck against the man's jaw, with a few sharp *crack* noises filling the night air. The pain grew stronger as I tried reaching out for anything to grab on to. I dropped to my knees holding my bump, I could feel a warm liquid covering my hands as I tried to stay awake, but my eyes felt so heavy, my head felt dizzy and my stomach slightly colder than the rest of my body. Soon, the music from inside had drowned out and all I heard was 2 gunshots sound out.

My body was moving faster than my mind. I only realized I was laying on the ground when my eyes caught a glimpse of the dark sky and my back felt uncomfortable against the gritty sidewalk. The discomfort was soon gone when my head was picked up and rested on someone's lap. His voice came as if far away in the distance, but the way he stroked my face and bump I knew it was Christian.

"Baby? Hey sweets, I'm sorry. I'm so sorry. You're gonna be okay." He kept repeating the words each time shakier than the last. I wanted to make one of my morbid jokes but I chose not to feeling his tears drop on my forehead, instead I tried to soothe him and let him know that I would be okay but I couldn't make out any words from the overflow of the same thick liquid I felt on my stomach, filling my mouth.

I closed my eyes just wanting to rest them for a minute, but I could hear Christian begging me not to, so I tried opening them to see his face again but once they were closed I couldn't keep my mind awake either. I'm not in any pain so I guess that's a plus, right?

JJ x

Chapter 25 - Too Perfect

T his chapter is dedicated to for always showing her love and support for this book xxYou guys should check out her work as well(Smut lovers can thank me later)

Christian

I felt his jaw shatter under my fist as I dealt vicious blows to his cheek. My rage was unrelenting after seeing him put his hands on her; even the warm blood sliding down my back, soaking through my shirt was no distraction for my anger. My knuckles kept delivering brutal attacks against his face until I stopped to pull my gun from my waist, leaving him to croak out his last words: "A son for a son."

It was only then that I noticed the trench knife attached to his hand and the blood dripping from its end.

I looked over to Alesha laying on the cold concrete looking up at the sky while her belly bled from different wound-sites through her white dress.

Without hesitation, keeping my focus on her, I shot the man twice between his eyes and went over to her limp body. Picking up her head, I placed it in my lap brushing the hairs from her face. I leaned forward kissing her forehead and softly rubbed her stomach which held our child. This was my fault. All of it.

"Baby? Hey sweets, I'm sorry. I'm so sorry. You're gonna be okay." My voice broke as my tears fell onto her. Maybe repeating the words would reassure her somehow, but I was trying to convince myself it was the truth. Blood started spouting from her lips as she tried to say something, but before she could, her eyes started drifting closed. I couldn't let her fall asleep. "Baby you can't close your eyes, okay? Just talk to me. A, please you can't close your eyes. Alesha talk to me."

She wouldn't open them. I could see her chest rise and fall but she wouldn't speak or open those big brown eyes for me. My head was still spinning from hitting it on the rock when he knocked me to the ground. I tried shaking away the dizziness and standing to my feet when a figure came rushing at us. I aimed my gun at the distorted frame, and just as quickly dropped it when I heard the person's voice.

"CHRIS! Come on we've gotta go! We need to get her to the hospital!" Antoni lifted her legs, helping me carry her to the back of the car. He quickly jumped into the driver's seat and pulled off.

"Dr Müeller, how fast can you get to Saints and Angels Hospital? Mr Marino has an emergency." Antoni spoke into the phone as he sped through the light traffic. "Good. Be prepped and waiting we should be there in 10 minutes or less."

The whole car ride my eyes wandered from her face to the bump that kept oozing that fucking blood. Her body laid out across my lap and the seats, paling and lifeless. I kept talking to her hoping she could hear me, but the lump in my throat trapped my voice to a faint whisper.

When we got to the hospital, Dr Müeller was already stood outside waiting with 5 nurses by his side and a gurney in front of them. I laid her body down and followed as they headed inside for the gray double doors down the hall.

Doc stopped and turned to me, pleading in his thick German accent "Mr Marino, you'll have to stay out here and trust me to do my job." I nodded hesitantly and watched as the doors shut behind them, my eyes staying anchored to it imagining she would come out smiling and unscathed in the next few minutes.

"Sir, you've been hurt. Come with me and I can check that out for you, then maybe you can answer some questions about what happened?"

I said nothing, felt nothing. It wasn't until the nurse put her hand on me that I felt the anger and irritation burgeoning. "Unless I ask for your help, I don't need it."

"Sir, you're bleeding from a head wound, that needs dressing, and an incident like this usually requires a report."

"My wife is bleeding out on a table and you think I'm in the mood to fill out paperwork, giving y'all some shit to gossip about?"

"That's not at all what I meant. I just thought-"

"I really don't give a shit what you thought. Get the fuck out of my face."

"Look, I'm just trying to do my job. If you don't want to pass out on my floors, someone should really look at that head wound."

"Lady, if you don't get the fuck out of my face in the next 2 seconds-"

Antoni cut me off, grabbing the hand that was already reaching for my gun. "Ma'am, I'll take over from here. Thank you." He smiled at the bitch as she walked back to her station with a scowl on her face. "I know you're mad but shooting up the hospital won't help anything, least of all Alesha."

Suddenly feeling all energy drain from me, I sat in the closest chair, eyes trained back on those gray doors.

-

Some time had passed and I still couldn't shift my stare. I could feel my family pacing and talking around me but it's like every sound was diluted to focus on the creak the door would make each time it swung open. It had already made that sound so many times making my heart race at 1000mph just to crash when it wasn't her or her doctors.

I've never believed in God but if he's real would he take them from me as punishment? Would he take her from me? Is this karma for all the bad shit I've done in my life? Was he patiently waiting for me to find something I couldn't live without just so he could rip it from me? I couldn't argue that I don't deserve that kind of pain, but I'd fight a thousand times over to prove that she didn't.

The obscure squeaking sound of the door caught my attention once again, this time the older man walked through in a fresh white lab coat. I stood, making my way over to him, already impatient from my wait. "How are they?"

"Well, we were able to control the bleeding and suture the wound sites, but Miss Moore must have taken a nasty hit to the head or had quite a devastating fall causing a swelling in the brain, so we've had to put her under a medically induced coma to help with management and recovery." The doctor, seemingly stressed or tired, took off his glasses to rub his eyes before putting them back on to finish his update. "Mr Marino.. I'm afraid the lacerations made to Miss Moore's abdomen were too deep to bypass the fetus."

I could hear Grams' breath shiver at the news, then Dani's soft muffled cries, supposedly into Rafael's chest. I tried pushing down everything I was feeling, but it all wanted to surface. Every tear, every harrowing cry, the numbness of my legs giving way beneath me. I willed it all aside to ask for the one thing I needed right now.

"I need to see her." My voice sounded unrecognizable. The grit, the exhausted and debilitated tone, none of it sounded like me.

"Right this way." Dr Müeller turned around making his way back through the double doors as I followed closely behind him.

We stopped in front of the spacious hospital room lit only by the sun's rays, I didn't realize it was already morning. I closed the door and walked further into the room toward the sound of the beeping machines. She was propped up on a few pillows, which was probably better for her recovery, but I knew she would hate it; she could never sleep comfortably with too many pillows. The tubes flowing from her mouth and arms made me wish this was one of her sadistic jokes, but it isn't. This is what happened because she decided to be with me. I took the seat next to her bed and lifted the small hand that fit perfectly in mine.

The beeps filled the silence for a while before I mustered the words to say what I was thinking.

"You know I hated you for a while after you left. Tried convincing myself you were weak and that I could find someone better who wouldn't fight me on everything every step of the way. How fucking stupid does that shit sound? Someone better than the Alesha Moore. It took me a while to figure out that I didn't hate you because you were weak, I just couldn't stand the fact that you were brave enough to walk away. I used to hate how you make me feel insecure and completely loved by you at the same time; how you make me second guess everything but still feel like any decision I make is the right one; how you believe in me wholeheartedly, but still call me on my bullshit. How you trusted me." My voice broke at the memory of all the promises I made. "I hated that the minute I met you I already knew you were all I wanted. I hated that for years I built this life prepared to never be completely happy then you changed that and tried taking it away from me. Truth is, I hate that I love you because you were right, you aren't built for my world. You're too good. Too perfect."

JJ x

Chapter 26 - Why Are You Here?

C hristian

"Sweetheart why don't you go home and take a shower? Maybe try eating something and get some sleep? You haven't eaten in days, you look so tired, and you still have.."

Grams' eyes travelled down to my chest causing me to look down at my dress shirt smeared with dried blood. Seeing the stained fabric made my pounding headache beat a little harder. She was probably right, I must look like shit especially given that I haven't slept the past 3 days. "I'm not leaving, I don't want her waking up here alone."

"She won't be alone. I'll be here til Danielle takes over later and then you can come back and spend the night. Christian, you won't be able to take care of her if you can't take care of yourself."

"Could you just ask Raf to bring something for me to change into and I'll take a shower here." She glanced at me pitifully, her eyes begging me to listen to her advice. Everyone who's come by to visit A has been sending me that same frustrating stare, as if this was her end and she was gone, but mostly because they probably blame me just as much as I do. "Grams, I appreciate what you're trying to do but just.. please."

"I'll make sure somebody gets you a change of clothes. Do you want something to drink or maybe I can order some of those tacos Alesha bought from that food truck? You loved those." I didn't give her an answer or move from my position, just waited for the talking to end. "I'll get some in case you change your mind."

I just wanted to be alone with A, so I was relieved when Grams' heels started making their way to the door. That's until I heard the commotion happening outside. I shot up and stepped in front of her heading toward the noise.

Opening the door, I watch as the tall, scrawny, disheveled man stood in front of Dominic demanding he move out of the way and allow him into the room.

I spoke out already annoyed at the idea of them disturbing Alesha in some way. "What's going on out here?"

"I don't know who any of you are, but the nurses told me the person I'm looking for is in this room and I'd be grateful if y'all would get the hell outta my way and mind your own business."

"Sir, I think you've got the wrong room. This is a private suite for one patient." His clothes hung off of his chalky brown skin which looked as if he had been constantly scratching at it. His pupils were dilated, casting a shade, making his eyes look almost entirely black.

"Devon?! What are you doing here?" As soon as Dani had rounded the corner her voice bellowed through the halls gaining everyone's attention. "Why are you here?!" She repeated the question with more force and disdain in her voice, letting me know this man wasn't a friend but a threat, one I wasn't risking.

I grabbed him by his arm and dragged him into the room, raising my gun to his head. "Dani, am I pulling the trigger or not?"

She didn't say anything, just looked on at the older man as if mentally weighing my question. After a moment of staring the man down, Dani finally spoke "Answer the question or leave. Don't do either and he will shoot you where you stand. Why are you here?"

"Girl don't talk to me like you grown. Y'all got caught up in all this mess running round here with these little boys playing house and look where she at now. Laid up in a hospital bed cause she followed yo fast ass. You probably the one got her into all this. Got some white boy pointing shit in my face like he know who I am." I pressed the gun harder against his temple desperate to get this over with. "She ain't changed her emergency contact since high school. They called, so we came."

"I don't know what type of game you're playing or what you're trying to get from her, but you need to leave. Now. Both of you."

"I ain't going nowhere. She gon need us when y'all get bored."

"Since when have you ever cared about anyone but yourself. If this is another one of your scams to guilt her into something, I will kill you myself. Chris I don't care what you do with him just don't have him in this room with her, especially not by himself."

"Dani who the fuck is this guy?"

"Devon Carter, the man I told you about. Ms Esther's dealer, the piece of shit A sold her necklace to pay."

"Hey now, that wasn't my fault. I gotta make my bread. Not like I tricked her out or nothin-"

I slipped the gun from his temple to his mouth. "Say one more fucking thing. I dare you."

A knock sounded at the door as Dominic opened it and told us a woman was trying to get by claiming she was Alesha's mom. Dani gave him a nod and before long the woman stepped into the room. Her dark unblemished skin was smooth, her eyes a shade of green lighter than my own and her frame small and frail.

"Danielle.. why am I not surprised? Seems like you're always right by her side when the bad shit is happening. Tell this white boy to step off my man."

"What do you want Esther? She isn't giving you any more money."

"I'm not here for no money, I'm here for my child. They called so I came, like any loving mother would. You always were a cold hearted little bitch, just like your mother."

"Hold up now." Grams put her purse down on the couch, stepping forward toward the other woman. "I'm gonna need for you to watch your mouth when you're talking to my kids. A big mouth won't get you far if you ain't got the hands to prove it."

Esther brought her focus back to Dani, a grimace etched on her face. "My daughter was in some mess most likely cause of knowing you. I'm here to strike some sense into her and get her right. I don't care what kinda new beginnings y'all think you had. It's over. I want you all out."

I swing my gun in her direction leaving it pointed in the middle of her head. "And who the fuck do you think you are?"

"According to the hospital and the law: her next of kin. That means what I say goes."

Before another breath was let out, the doors opened again, with hospital security barging in and ordering all non family members to leave the room.

The head of security walked over to me tentatively, explaining himself. "Mr Marino, I understand your position, but it's also hospital policy to adhere to the family's wishes." I dropped my hand, putting the gun back in my waistband and keeping my eyes locked on Esther's.

"That's fine. Alesha's family wishes for these two to be escorted from the premises and banned unless in need of medical aid."

With a nod, the security guard started steering Devon out of the room. He reached for Esther, but she pulled out ID shoving it in the guard's face. "He can't do that, I'm her mother! You can't do this!" She yelled looking to me.

"Next of kin gets to make the calls, isn't that what you said?" I questioned her with incredulous sarcasm.

"The staff here have already been informed that I'm Alesha's husband, Dani's her sister and Winnie is her grandmother. I'm sure they'll trust the word of a ward donor before they believe a couple smack-heads. You could always fight me on this, but is that the road you wanna go down? I haven't got a lot of patience these days and Grams always did say creativity influences idle hands; in my line of business that's not always a good thing."

JJ x

Chapter 27 - White Boy

C hristian

She's supposed to be awake by now. It's been two and a half weeks and there haven't been any changes. Being so focused on A meant I didn't have the energy or time to deal with Esther; who had been coming back to the hospital everyday with outcries to see her daughter. So, to put an end to all her constant nagging and threats, I allowed her to visit under the circumstances that she doesn't bring that guy back with her and she stayed out of everybody's way. If I knew, beyond a shadow of a doubt, that Alesha wouldn't care, this woman would already be 6 feet under.

Even after fighting so hard to get these visits, Esther would only show up for 10 minutes every morning to check if Alesha had woken up, then leave immediately after seeing there was no change.

Today was different. Today she stayed. Sitting slumped in the chair at Alesha's bed side opposite me, she had a slight manic expression in her eyes. I held A's hand a little tighter not trusting how close to us she was.

"You know what white boy? You not even that bad. You the one that got her this room right? You the one that got her pregnant too? Have to be, otherwise you doing a little too much for some pussy." I stared at her unbothered by her bullshit as she let out a cackle and continued. "Judging by that gun you held to my head and keep on your hip, you probably the reason she ain't pregnant now."

I clenched my free hand into a fist at my side and tried to keep calm as my knee started bouncing erratically which only happened when my anger was getting the best of me. My heart pounded against my chest forcing me to take deep breaths.

"I got a little bit of advice for you white boy: leave this one alone. I told her a long time ago that families weren't for us, she should've listened. That thing is better off where it is now than being raised by her."

The words stilled me. My heart stopped its hectic rhythm and fell to the pit of my stomach. My hold loosened on Alesha's hand but her palm stayed fixed in mine, my glare piercing Esther's mint green eyes. She sat up in her chair, nervousness clouding her features, knowing she went too far.

"I get it. You loved your husband til the day he died and then destroyed your daughter because there was no one else to blame. You broke her down, telling her all this bullshit about not being good enough for anyone, just so you wouldn't feel alone in the fact that no one wanted to be around you. But she did, at least she did back then. Isn't that crazy? A 12 year old needing the only parent they have left. We've talked about you ..and him: the man you brought here." The look in her eyes got more fearful as I kept going. "I know about everything you've done; both of you. I know the real reason she tried to take her life, and it wasn't because of that necklace, even though that's the explanation she gave Dani. Do you know why, at 15, your daughter thought she was better off dead?" My words came out harsh and bitter as I spoke on.

"Whatever she said was a lie. She was always dramatic in how she'd tell her stories."

"Do better than that, a liar is one thing she definitely is not." I looked at her through narrowed eyes, unimpressed by her lazy attempt at an excuse. "She paid him off and he left the house, but you begged him to come back later that night. Hadn't gotten your fix yet? You took some lines and got drunk, so while you were high off your ass he went to her room and tried creeping into the bed. She screamed for you, did you hear? She said you were too jaded to help her, but I'm not as trusting as she is." I kept staring her down, feeling a hatred for her grow the more I remembered what Alesha told me. "Did you even bat an eye when you heard her fighting him off? When she managed to lock herself in the bathroom, hiding for 7 hours, did checking on her even cross your mind? What about when she used that old razor on her wrists, where were you then?" Esther avoided my gaze, eyes darting around the room as her breaths came out in angry puffs. "She told me that that afternoon showed her what her life was going to be like with you in it and she couldn't imagine how else to get out. You failed her long before that night though. You realize that when your husband died, he was taken from both of you; instead you were so busy looking for him, you lost her too."

"You think you could offer her anything better? I loved my husband, hell, I still do. When he was gone I didn't see the point in living. I had a kid that I couldn't raise alone and a life I didn't want anymore, not without him. You think she's ever gonna be truly happy? Worrying about you every day and night? Is that fair to her? How will you feel leaving her to raise a family when someone finally cuts you down? Knowing the way things work in my neighbourhood, I'm surprised people ain't already tried coming for her to get to you. You love her so much? Get the hell out of her life."

I grit my teeth, trying to hold back the retort wanting to fly out of my mouth, because there's a part of me that agreed with her. She got up and headed for the door.

"All those things didn't happen because you couldn't cope, it's because you didn't try. She's better than us, she's forgiving. I'm not. That reminds me, don't get too fond of Mr Carter. Oh, and a little warning, I've let a lot of the things you've said about my family slide, but don't mistake that for weakness; push me far enough and I won't care whose mom you are." I relaxed in my chair still holding A's hand while the sounds of the machines filled the room before the door opened and closed behind me.

-

Alesha

"Hello?! Babe! Are you here?!" I shouted into Christian's empty house. There was no reply, just the echo of my voice ricocheting off the walls.

As I stepped further into the house everything started falling apart. The ceiling and columns fell as ashes around me. I stood motionless as the dust settled on the marble floor. When it did, I called out again for Christian. There was still no answer, instead, a faint groan sounded from where the kitchen used to be. Walking past the burnt cinders I made my way to the noise.

Ashes rained steadily in the decayed room, while a body laid flat on its back in the middle of it all. Moving closer, I noticed Christian's tattooed forearms through the dust clouds gathering faintly throughout the room. The circled area he lay in was brighter than the rest of the room; none of the falling debris had trickled into it. It was clean but he wasn't. He had soot and blood in patches all over his face and clothes. I tried running to him, but the harder I tried the further away he seemed to get.

That's when Vasiliev appeared, walking past me toward the clearing, he held a gun in his hand. He looked at Christian with a sneer before stepping into the circle and pointing the weapon at his head. I ran harder and faster, screaming and pleading with Vasiliev not to do it, but was forced to watch as he pulled the trigger on a powerless Christian.

In the blink of an eye I was stood in my childhood home with a baby in my arms and Devon sitting on the sofa. The house was eerily quiet, but in that instance I knew exactly what this meant. I'd fought so hard to leave only to end up right back here. A child to raise alone, an escape staring back at me from the couch, and no Christian to soothe my mind.

I jumped from my sleep in a cold sweat, heart racing, while Christian laid asleep at my side in our bed. Reaching over, I checked his pulse and inspected his face making sure there were no bruises like in the nightmare.

"Baby, what are you doing?" His chuckle and gruff sleepy voice felt like music to my ears.

Dropping back onto the pillow, I allowed my heart to relax knowing he was safe. My heavy breathing must've confused Christian as he sat up and turned the lamp on to see me with beads of sweat formed all over my face and neck and wearing a soaked through T-shirt.

"Shit! Are you okay?" Not waiting for a reply, he pressed the back of his hand to my forehead then shot up running to the bathroom and coming back with a cold cloth, to rest against my forehead. "Should we go to the hospital? Are you okay? Is this a thing for pregnant people? Maybe I should call Grams and check if this is normal."

"Christian it was a dream, I'm fine. I just need a second."

He ran over to the walk-in closet to get a pair of jeans and a hoodie, but the room fell silent. There was no more shuffling of his feet against the carpet, none of his worried mumblings, just silence. Anxiety shaking my nerves, I called out to him, no answer. I called once more and still, nothing. Getting up, I headed for the closet, but just as before, the minute I started moving, everything began crumbling to dust. Feeling exhausted, frustrated and helpless, I fell to my knees burying my face in my palms.

Suddenly strong arms wrapped around my shoulders, bringing me into a hard chest. I immediately felt at ease. It was him. His scent, his arms, his warmth. I could hear him whispering reassurances of me being okay and nothing happening to me. I felt myself drifting off to sleep.

-

The bright light shone against my eyes creating the most uncomfortable feeling. Opening my mouth to speak out, my throat felt sore and dry, so I closed it hoping to soothe the pain a little. I lazily dragged my hand over my stomach only to feel someone's head of hair strewn across my belly.

"A?! Hey baby. I'm here, I'm here. Dani can you go get the doctor, she's awake!"

JJ x

Chapter 28 - Three

The 3 men had grown impatient waiting for Christian to arrive. It had already been 15 hours since they'd been confined to this space, but all 3 knew his absence was more than likely Alesha related.

They had spent so long in the darkened room that they were now fully accustomed to the strong scent of bleach coating the area.

The idea of meeting with the biggest criminal on the East Coast, without regards to outside the US, put the grown men on edge. The oldest gentleman with graying hair and a beard to match, was calmly taking note of the items on the table in front of them. The youngest, who was a black man carrying a bold gold chain around his neck was evidently irritated, cussing to himself. While the other white man, who donned scars all over his visible skin, grinned to himself at their obvious tensity.

Although no words were said, each man scoped out the room with a wariness of everything and everyone occupying the space.

The rusting copper door creaked open as it brushed across the dirty concrete floor. Their attention darted to the direction of the sound, only to see Christian Marino DeLuca step into the room.

"Hello gentlemen. I apologize for the wait, although, I'm sure you're all familiar with my circumstances at the moment, which is also the reason I've brought you here." The men stared back at him in anticipation of how he would proceed. "Today is just an opportunity to resolve our pasts, on behalf of myself and my family. You've all earned this justice and I am a man of principle. However, I should note that I believe it's only a modicum of what you really deserve." Christian's eyes locked on the older gray haired man sat to the far right of the room.

"Shall we begin?" Shrugging off his suit jacket, he sent an innocent smile to the men.

He walked over to the table where different sharpened tools laid wait for his use. Running his hands along the tray of blades, he reached for the small scalpel that caught his eye. "Before that..", he halted his movements, turning back to the graying man, "I got you something". Christian strode over to his jacket, pulling a black box from its pocket; he made his way over to the man, lifting a syringe filled with clear liquid from the case. Slowly, but heedlessly, Christian pierced the exposed skin of the man's arm, injecting all the contents into his body.

The old man hissed at the discomfort and slight sting the needle caused. "Don't worry, it's just a little experiment our Irish friends whipped up; the sick bastards. You're the first to try it, so for all we know, it might not work." Christian shrugged as he walked back to the array of utensils; he put the syringe back in the box and threw it on the table.

He paced in front of the men, debating who should go first.

"ARRGGGHHHH! WHAT THE FUCK IS THIS!?!"

"Hmm, whaddya know, it works, and fast too. I'll let Dermot know." Christian smiled watching the old man fight against his restraints. Whatever Christian had given him caused every muscle in his body to burn and ache as if boiling him from the inside out. He writhed against the makeshift barbed-wire ropes Christian's men had tied him down with; creating deep cuts in his wrists and ankles that he was numb to because of the pain attacking his entire body.

Christian ignored his cries as his emerald eyes bounced between the other culprits: one laid out with his arms and legs strapped to the steel bed, while the other was chained to the ceiling by his wrists.

"Always were one for theatrics, weren't you Marino?" Vasiliev teased still grinning brightly as he tried to fight the nausea and soreness of having his arms in the air for so long.

"In that case, you must be a real Meryl Streep." Christian chuckled stepping towards him. "Showing up to my house, ordering my death, threatening to rape and murder my woman. All because I said I didn't wanna be friends." Christian said with a playful pout.

"You're wasting your time, you've got bigger enemies than us. Let me go; I'll head back to Russia and you won't hear from me again, otherwise my people will come looking, I've made many powerful allies, Christian; I'm Bratva."

"*tsk tsk tsk* Ivan, are you threatening me?" Ivan shook his head laughing at Christian's fearless persona, but the smile on Christian's face only grew. "In this business loyalty can be bought. You're men needed a leader and you were busy running from me, what do you think happened?" Ivan's head rose as he stared at Christian in disbelief. "What was it you said that night? "At least your men have yet to betray you"?" He mocked the helpless man, laughing at his shaken reaction. "In fact.." Christian strolled over to the only other chair in the sparse room and took a seat. "Vince! KC! Harlem!"

Another 3 men walked into the room making Vasiliev's eyes widen. The muscular black man ambled with a sledgehammer in tow, the slender white guy who was covered in tattoos swung a machete by his side and the tall, well built Asian man, whose perfectly tailored suit made him stand out from the group, carried a pair of spiked knuckle dusters in his fist.

"Are these the powerful allies who were to come looking for me, Ivan?"

"What are you all doing here?!" He noticed the remorseful expression each man held on his face, but even worse he knew what that meant for him. "You don't have to do what he says! Kill him and free me! I'm Bratva! My men are still loyal!"

"Don't have to do what I say? Your contempt is knocking my ego, Ivan." Chris held his chest feigning hurt. "You'd never stand for that kind of disrespect, would you?" Ivan raised his chin trying to hold his head high and appear braver than he felt. "Bring me 3 of his fingers." Christian kept his eyes on Vasiliev as he ordered the men.

Making his way to Ivan, KC pulled a blade from his holster. He reached up examining the fingers before asking the angry Russian: "Which one's do you wanna keep?"

"What the fuck do you think you're-"

KC swung the blade, slashing Ivan's pinky, ring and middle fingers, before handing the bloodied digits over to Christian, who threw them callously to the floor behind him. Wiping the blood from his blade onto his hand-kerchief, KC took his place next to his partners.

Vasiliev wept from the pain as his hope for survival died. "See Ivan, you should've made better friends." Christian mocked shaking his head. "Say hi to Sebastian. Kill him. But do it slowly, no weapons." The men dropped their items to the ground. As KC removed his jacket and dress shirt, Christian saw the glint of his gold knuckle dusters and motioned for him to bring them. "I'll get these back to you." KC gave him a nod before joining the other 2 men who had already began their savage attack on the wailing Russian.

-

After the men were done with Vasiliev, his entire body was unrecognizable. Christian watched the whole thing unfazed, even taking part in the mauling at some points. He didn't seem to mind being soaked in the blood, whereas the sight and smell of Ivan's blood, innards and marred skin had even the ones doing the harm, wincing. Though they still pushed through, fearing the consequences of stopping. Vince, Harlem and KC were eager to leave the warehouse after carrying out Christian's commands; taking one last look at the battered body, they made a swift exit.

"1 down, 2 to go. Now we're alone, who wants to go next?" The two men kept quiet, but their hearts raced in their chests at the mere memory of Ivan's screams ringing throughout the very same room not too long ago. "Don't both volunteer at once." Christian quipped with another chilling chuckle.

Choosing a broad kitchen knife from the tray, Christian walked over to Devon laying on the autopsy table. Carter's cocky manner had long faded, he was honestly the most terrified he'd ever been, but fuck if he would let this maniac in front of him know that.

Christian snatched the chain from Carter's neck before running the knife from his throat to his widows peak.

"Look man, I'm not part of this. I don't even fucking know you! That bitch just showed up and said come to New York and we'd get paid big. I won't even take a cut, Esther can have it all." Devon pleaded.

Esther won't be getting any money, not from us."

"I'm not talking about y-"

"Mr Carter, I don't like you. Frankly, calling you a spineless piece of shit doesn't even scratch the surface. Of course, this is all from a biased perspective, but a suiting statement wouldn't you agree?" Chris looked up to see the older man in the corner with his eyes trained on his lap, avoiding the scene in front of him. Probably trying to control the pain flowing through his body; the distress was evident on his face.

"Do you not like the show? I thought you lived for this stuff? Once in a lifetime experience, especially considering this is literally the last of your lifetime." The man sat quietly, eyes still focused on his lap. "I know what will get your attention."

Christian marched over to the man's chair, undoing his belt as he went. Holding the panel, he whipped the leather, sending a thunderous *whack* across the older man's cheek with the buckle. "Hey, pick your head up."

He raised his head, blood now falling from his temple. "WHAT DO YOU WANT?!"

"It's no fun if you're gonna be a grouch." Christian tied the belt around the old man's neck, latching it through the slats of the chair, leaving him sat in an upright position. He made his way back over to the table and played with the tools for a while before taking it back to the old man. He pleaded and begged as Christian forced his eyes open, lining up his makeshift contraption to the old man's lower lashes.

"There you go! Try not to blink." Christian said with a devilish grin, condescendingly slapping the old man's cheek.

He went back to Devon, picking up the knife. Without pausing, he struck the blade against Devon's arm, frowning at the lack of impact it had as the man's yells echoed throughout the room.

"Dominic!" The giant came tumbling into the room, sneering at the old man sitting in the corner.

"Yes, boss?"

"Do you have Bluebell with you?"

"Always, boss."

Christian held his hand out while Dome drew the sleek black mini axe with a shining silver sharp blade from his waist, placing it in his boss's palm.

In one sudden move, Christian had brought the axe down on Devon's left knee severing his lower leg from his body. He flailed and writhed against the straps holding him down. His screams melding with the old man's as he had shut his eyes. Their combined cries ripped through the room bouncing off of the concrete walls.

Christian held the knife to Dome and motioned to Devon's body. Dome nodded, understanding Christian's order. Standing by his head, Dominic began a deep incision from Devon's left ear, across his forehead, all the way to his right. The man's screams were deafening but Dome was amused by how high pitched he was getting. Christian had already forced the other man's eyes back open, leaving him to sit with a mixture of blood and tears spilling down his cheeks.

Taking his place back at Dome's side, Chris locked eyes with a panicking Devon. "At least I'm not using an.. I don't know.. razor" he said sarcastically with a straight face, before hammering bluebell against the table again, this time removing one of Devon's arms. Carter's screams quickly died out as his body went limp. Dome checked his pulse and shook his head.

"Boss, his heart just gave out. We can try and resuscitate if you wanna finish?"

"Nah, he's too much of a pussy, it'd probably just give out again. Got-dammit! Carter, you fucking asshole, couldn't even die properly!" Christian struck the axe once more, making a clean slice through Devon's neck. "Sorry about Bluebell."

Christian handed Dome the axe, the black wooden handle was drenched in blood coating the engraving: 'I can't promise to be here for the rest of your life, but I can promise to love you for the rest of mine. Maya x'. The axe was Dominic's most treasured possession from his wife, named 'Bluebell' after her favourite flower. "Don't be, it's what she's for." He'd used it for much worse.

Christian turned his attention to the old man, hearing his tear-filled pleas float through the empty room.

"Last, but certainly not least." Christian walked over to him, removing the small needles from his lids, making his sobs dwindle. "You are a grown fucking man, act like it!" Christian moved behind the chair and began pulling on the belt wrapped around the old man's neck. He coughed and sputtered, choking as he was dragged backwards into a rusting bathroom.

Christian released his grip, giving some relief to the man's throat. It wouldn't last long. Dome helped Christian lift the chair into the bathtub which was filled with ice cold water. His feet plunged into the freezing substance, making the man begin to shiver.

"Call the crew to organise clean up." Dome took his orders and pulled out his cellphone dialling a number as he left the room.

"How're you feeling Julian?" Christian asked with narrowed eyes.

"I've made my choices and stand by them. I refused to let you're crimes go unpunished." Julian's teeth chattered as he spoke with a clenched jaw.

"Your son was a gutless, disloyal coward, he deserved what happened to him. If anything, I was too nice; I should've locked him down here for a while, give Dominic something to do. You really think that poor excuse of a soldier earned the respect you're giving him?"

"Yes. Sebastian was my son-"

"HE WASN'T WORTH THE LIFE OF MINE!" Christian's words bellowed through the small room as his voice trembled. "Your son betrayed your name when he betrayed me. You should've accepted that, at the very most you should've limited your hit to my life only. But you didn't. You sent that man for my girl and unborn child." Feeling tears burn the back of his eyes, Christian rubbed his temples soothing his anger.

"With this life, no one is untouchable. You knew what dangers you put them in, that is no one's blame but you're own. A son for a son Mr Marino."

Christian saw the impenitent look on Julian's face as he spoke. All hate and disdain for the man came flooding back. He balled his fist and landed a mind-numbing punch, which was shortly followed by a *crack* signaling Julian's nose breaking as his chair flew back submerging his head and torso fully under the cold water. His body shook as he tried but failed to breathe; his feet and hands thrashed at the ankles and wrists fighting against the metal holding him down, only creating deeper wounds from the razor-edged threads of wire.

Christian stood watching his body flail for a while before dragging him back up. Christian drew one of the knuckle-dusters from his back pocket, attaching it to his hand before throwing punch after punch, piercing Julian's skin.

Every time he got winded he would throw Julian back into the water, almost drowning him before bringing him back to the surface and delivering more blows to his body. It didn't take long for his begging and sobs to turn into unintelligible garble.

-

The crew were already in the other room using acid to dissolve Vasiliev and Carter's bodies in tanks. Christian pulled the plug on the tub and waited for the water to drain out, then put the stopper back in place. Laying Julian down, he turned around and left the bathroom.

Seconds later 4 burly men walked in wearing thick rubber gloves and carrying their own heavy tanks. They looked to Christian, who stood at the door, for one last nod as permission.

They slowly dumped the tanks of acid over Julian's body, witnessing him screech and struggle against the chair as his skin, muscles and bones melted away. He continued screaming, gargling and choking on the chemicals, until he couldn't. Christian walked out removing his blood-soaked shirt, throwing it over to the mess the men had collected.

"You ready, boss?" Dome asked, hoping Christian was done. He was set to leave as the bleak tunnels had began stinking from the dead corpses.

Christian walked past him with a saddened expression, exhausted by the hours spent in that room but content with the idea that now those men were dealt with, he could get back to his family. "Let's go."

JJ x

Update: I've decided to split Becoming His into a 2 part series. That way I can publish part 1 and dedicated readers can see Christian and Alesha's ending on Wattpad in part 2

Chapter 29 - Broken Birdie

~

"He's dead." Christian's eyes darted to Alesha's sullen face as she unexpectedly broke from the lighthearted conversation that had gradually filled the room of their friends and family. "Isn't he?"

The quiet was overwhelming as everyone's gaze tightened on her tired eyes. She had been awake now for 7 hours but Christian had already instructed everyone, even Dr Müeller, to avoid that topic until he had a chance to explain everything. The doctor had warned him of how exhausted and out of sorts she would be for the first few hours, so it only made sense to Chris to stray from the news of their son until he was sure she could handle it.

Everyone couldn't stop talking about how grateful they were that she was okay and had finally woken up, but she could see something different in each person. The way Grams kept herself in a chair to one corner of the room with saddened red eyes. The fact that every time they locked sight, Dani would leave the room on the verge of tears with Raf chasing after her.

Even Gramps, who had hugged her for so long, dropped a few tears on her shoulder before breaking away. But the biggest giveaway, Christian.

The same man who, for the last 5 months hadn't shut up about how cool of a dad he would be and the adventures he'd already planned with his "mini-me", didn't say a word. Not even asking the doctor how the baby was. He sat in the leather hospital chair on her right, hand cemented in her palm the whole time not saying a thing.

"Let's give these two the room." Vincenzo stood to his feet reaching out for Winnie's hand before leading everyone else out of the tense hospital room.

"Who did it?" She asked, turning her attention to the natural light shining through the floor to ceiling window. Christian couldn't answer, still taken aback by her abrupt approach, he tried stringing together the right words to put her at ease without lies, but he couldn't. His silence was enough for her. "Who was it?" She asked again, her tone emotionless.

"Julian Howard."

"Is he dead?"

"Not yet."

"I need him to be."

Christian gazed at her skeptically, she didn't sound the same. Her soft spoken demeanour was gone. Her questions came out stony and detached, almost militant. She wasn't herself, but he'd be damned if he didn't give her the justice she deserved.

"Done."

~

That was a week ago. After killing Julian Howard, Christian had hoped Alesha would feel some relief as she eased back into her old self, but he was wrong. There was no more smiling and she'd barely spoken to anyone except Winnie since that day. With everything that's happened, he hadn't even seen her shed a tear yet. Her time bounced between looking out to the city from her room and whispered chats with Winnie when no one else was around.

His grandmother refused to tell him what the topics of conversation were and instead explained how losing a child can change a mother and that it will take a while for her to feel like herself again. He understood, but it didn't stop him from feeling like he'd already lost Alesha too. He'd convinced himself that, while the people around them would never say it, they blamed him; and every second spent around her, he was in his own head wondering if she blamed him too.

-

She was finally leaving the hospital today which Christian had been looking forward to. He had high hopes that familiar surroundings would speed up the process of getting back to normal, so his impatience for them to leave that room was immense.

"Great. Just follow the light for me." The doctor instructed, aiming the small flashlight at her eyes. "You should be very proud of the progress you've made Miss Moore, it's nothing short of impressive." She gave him a small smile, fidgeting with her hands. I will set up a few home visits for you just to ensure you're recovery stays on track. Remember, no work for the next 2 weeks, take it easy and focus on your PT. Other than that, I'll be seeing you in a few days time. Any questions?"

She sent the older man another friendly smile that didn't reach her eyes. "No questions. Thank you Dr Müeller."

"Thanks doc." Christian walked him to the door shaking his hand before he left. As he walked back to grab Alesha's bags, the door opened behind him.

"What are you doing here?" Alesha asked the unexpected visitor with wide eyes and a shaky voice.

With all the chaos happening in their lives after Alesha had woken up, Christian had forgotten to mention the fact that her mother had been here. Esther's absence since the last time he'd seen her, made him think she decided to cut her visit short. He was wrong.

"Didn't your little boyfriend tell you I came looking for you when the hospital called?" Alesha looked to Christian, embarrassed by her past, hoping he hadn't drawn any similarities in the 2 women since meeting her mother; a look he distressingly misconstrued as disappointment in him. "I need to talk to you. Leave us alone." Making her way over to her daughter, Esther motioned to Chris to leave the room.

"What are you doing? You don't get to come into my life demanding anything. You don't get that kind of power."

"Little girl, you need to watch your mouth. You not too old to get popped." Esther's sneer made Alesha scoff at the aged woman.

"Goodbye Esther." Standing to her feet, Alesha grabbed Christian's arm and headed for the door.

While trying to pass Esther, her mother clutched her arm, halting her steps. "Birdie, please. I'm begging you." Alesha hadn't heard that nickname since her dad passed. The words made her heart skip a beat. "Just 5 minutes.. please."

Alesha looked at her mother's glowering face and felt vague pity for the woman. Letting go of Christian's arm, she asked him to give them a minute alone. Although he'd left the room, he stood at the door straining his ears to listen in on the private talk. Through the muffled speech he only managed to make out what Esther was saying, and that's only because she was talking like someone in a crowded bar trying to talk over the music.

"You know he killed Devon? You need to leave him. Come back home with me, I'm better now."…"After everything I've done for you, you'd throw me to the side for some white boy who makes a living as a murderer?!" Christian rolled his eyes but carried on listening. "You may not want me around but you know everything I'm saying is the truth."…"Look at your life right now and tell me he's good for you. Has anything good happened for you since you two got together?" Another strong wave of guilt and shame overtook his emotions as he heard the harsh truths Esther doled out.…"That's dead and gone. Try again." Suddenly a loud clap sounded through the door followed by a shriek. Christian opened the door ready to put an end to whatever was happening when he saw Alesha's eyes welling up and Esther on the floor cupping her cheek.

"You don't ever let so much as a peep come out of your mouth about my son. We're done, Christian let's go."

In the time he'd known her, Alesha had never been violent to anyone or anything, no matter how annoyed she was, so her reaction was a shock to him. Deserved, but still shocking. He felt proud of her for standing up to the woman who'd caused her so much stress and pain, but irked that this growth seemed to veer further and further away from who she actually was.

-

They had made it to the hospital parking lot and were sitting in the car waiting for the unusual awkward tension between them to slip away ahead of the drive. "Birdie?" Her eyes narrowed on him as a smirk broke out on her face. He grinned at the sight of playfulness gracing her face, a sight he had been missing desperately.

"I was hoping you didn't catch that. It's not that interesting."

"Too bad, I've gotta know now."

Still smiling, she let out a deep sigh. "When I was younger, my dad took my mom and I to this bird sanctuary, and in the first 5 minutes I was already obsessed with the little creatures. So, later when he asked me what I wanted to be when I grew up, it felt only right to say "a birdie". He never let it go and the name's stuck with me since." A chuckle left her lips at the memory she'd buried in the back of her mind.

"I like it, it suits you." Christian started up the car before looking back over to Alesha. Her face was turned away from him, to the window, but he could see the tears gathering on her lower lashes. Just as fast as he felt he'd gotten her back, he'd lost her again.

***

As soon as they'd gotten back to Christian's, Alesha was so exhausted, she made a bee-line for the bedroom.

Lately, being around Christian, all she felt was an overwhelming sense of remorse. Shame that she somehow wasn't strong enough to protect their child: even though deep down she knew there was probably nothing she could do; and then there was the distress of what she asked him to do after: she regretted ever asking him to take another person's life, putting that moral pressure on him. Maybe the feeling would fade after a while, but for now she just needed to sleep.

"Hey," Christian tugged her arm towards him before she could get any further into the house, "do you need anything?" Her distance was truly starting to worry him.

She gave him a tired smile and shook her head, "no, I just need to take a nap."

"I love you. You know that right?" His eyes locked on hers trying to figure out what she wasn't saying to him.

"I love you too." Her words said something that her face and body wasn't relaying. Placing a soft kiss on his lips, she slipped out of his hold, making her way upstairs.

-

After spending 15 minutes in his office trying to focus, Christian gave up on the work sitting in front of him and headed upstairs to have the talk they both needed. Getting closer to their bedroom door he could hear sobs and muffled sniffling. He walked in to see Alesha sat on the edge of the bed crying into the blue baby blanket he'd bought for their son.

He remembered how he'd roll his eyes at how much she bought in preparation, while secretly hiding his own collection for the newborn. He had forgotten to clear the drawer he kept them in.

She cried harder, unable to hold back everything she'd been feeling and suppressing the past week, "I.. I-I just.. C-Chris-". Her voice was broken. Her heart was broken. She was broken.

He walked over and helped her into bed, climbing in behind her; hugging her into him. He felt her body shaking as he squeezed her to his chest hoping he could take her pain away, but knowing that wasn't possible. His chest was heavy with a burden of self-reproach, that doubled in size seeing her this way. Holding her in his arms until she had fallen asleep, he buried his head in her curls, finally understanding what she truly needed.

JJ x

Chapter 30 - Losing Everything

WARNING: MATURE SCENEREAD AT YOUR OWN DISCRETION

Alesha

I sat up in bed listening to the calming patter of the running shower. There must be something on his mind; Christian never wakes up this early without spending at least 30 minutes on his phone playing videos trying to 'accidentally' wake me up and make me keep him company while he got ready. He was definitely in his head and it was most likely my fault. I know I've been distant lately but last night helped. All the crying probably had my eyes looking red and puffy, but I felt better not holding it all in like I had been.

I was so wrapped in my own thoughts that I hadn't realized the shower stopped, not until he walked out of the bathroom with a towel tightly folded around his waist. He looked up, meeting my eyes with his clear green ones, but they showed no emotion. He didn't wear his standard smile or a sexy smirk, nothing.

Instead, he broke his gaze and headed for the walk-in closet. "Morning, I didn't mean to wake you."

"You didn't, I guess I just wasn't as tired as I thought." I called out a little louder, my throat still slightly sore.

Nothing. No quips, no conversation. His silence was new and unsettling. I was usually pissed that I could never get him to stop talking in the mornings, but right now I was missing the familiar routine. He walked back into the open space with his shoes and suit pants already on, buttoning up the crisp white dress shirt. He went around the room collecting more than his daily items, seemingly trying.. to ignore me?

"Are you okay? Like.. are we okay? Is something wrong?"

He looked up, finally acknowledging me again, his eyes still holding a steely expression. Quickly dropping the cold stare, he inhaled deeply running a hand down his face. His eyes were fixed to the floor for a while, like he was hypnotized by the shaggy white carpet.

"Christian? Are-"

"Esther was right." His focus shifted to me. "Julian Howard was right." My chest tightened at the mention of the man's name. "Hell, you were right." My brows furrowed in confusion at what he was getting at. "We shouldn't be together; we need to end this." The words weren't quite sinking in as he started packing everything into the bag I just noticed sitting at the foot of the bed. "I'm leaving tonight to settle some business in LA, so I'll be gone a couple days, Antoni and Dominic will take you to look at some places this week. If you find something you like, put an offer down and I'll take care of it. I would leave you the mansion but I know you're not too fond of how empty it feels on your own. I've set up a monthly transfer to your accou-"

"Stop! I'm not sure I'm getting this, what the hell are you talking about?" I threw the covers to the side, shuffling out of the bed, getting closer to him so I don't mistake the words coming out of his mouth.

"We're done, Alesha." He sounded vexed by the conversation that only just started; almost like he'd already debated it with himself. "If you need more than what I've arranged th-"

"Chris! Shut up for a second." I rest my hand on my hip and closed my eyes, balling my other fist against my forehead, in an attempt to wrap my head around his foolishness. "What are you doi- why are you doing this?" The frustration was now leaking into my voice. "If you need time, I can stay at my apartment, but if this is you making rash decisions over what's happened then just stop for a second and talk to me."

He shoved a piece of clothing into the bag turning back to me with a wild look in his eyes. "Rash?! Can you honestly say you won't resent me if something like this happens again?! Because as much as I try to keep you safe I feel like I'm failing at every turn!" Seeing the way his roar startled me, he soothed his anger and lowered his voice. "You should've left that night. After Dani told you who I was you should've fucking run."

"Well, I didn't then and I won't now. I love you, Christian." I reached up, brushing my palm against his cheek. Pulling his head down to mine, I looked into the comforting emerald orbs with hopes that the thoughts speeding through his mind would wane for just a minute. Releasing a despondent sigh, he backed away, packing the rest of his things into the bag and zipping it up.

-

The argument kept going back and forth, each of us trying to suppress our ire with the situation, until we were both at our wits end.

"I can't pull you back into this, we've already lost so much. You've already lost too much. We both have to accept what needs to happen. Why are you making this so hard?"

"Hard?! This is me not trying to lose everything, Christian!" I shouted through the rasp in my voice, too exhausted and frustrated to hold back the tears streaming down my face. "You told me that you'd fight for me and I'm trying to do the same!" I could see his own tears stacking on the rim of his eyes, but nothing fell. "Are you really doing this?" Everything in me hoped he would drop this whole conversation and we'd go back to bed, because it was way too early for my life to fall apart; but nothing prepared me for the reality settling in.

He picked up the bag and started walking toward the door. "Antoni and Dominic should be here soon, like I said, let me know if you ever need me to send more-"

My jaw slacked at his callous attitude. "I don't need your house or your money." The words rattled through my tears. Making my way to the bathroom, I slammed the door needing to stop the flood of tears and quell the rage surging through my veins. Taking the time to breathe and compose myself only took a few minutes, but by the time I stepped out, he was already gone. Just like that we were done.

*****

I tapped my champagne flute, getting everyone's attention. Clearing my throat, I began the short speech that had taken me way too long to write.

"Danielle Prudence Taylor-"

"Girl, I love you, but don't try me." She quipped, breaking my roll.

I chuckled before continuing, "21 years I've known you and for all 21 you've had my back through everything. Meeting you on that playground, hustling kids out of their pudding cups, was the best thing to ever happen to me. You've been a mother, a sister and a best friend all wrapped in a thic package."

"Two C's?", she jokingly asked wiping away the tears slipping down her cheek.

"Five. Now let me finish. ..I'm so proud you chose Rafael to be by your side, and though he'll be cheering you on in everything you do, I will still be here to hold you up when he gets tired. You both truly deserve the love, respect and happiness you give to one another. Congratulations you guys. I love you mama." She blew me a kiss from across the table, mouthing an 'I love you'.

Taking my seat while everyone raised their glasses and cheered, I checked my phone and smiled at the text that had just come in. Sending one back, I can't help but feel a certain someone's eyes on me. I'd been dreading the small post-wedding get together since helping Dani and Grams plan the thing, but it seemed to be going well.

Dani stood up, clearly already a little tipsy. "Thank you so much to all of you for making it out tonight. We really wanted to celebrate with the people we love the most and y'all made the cut. At least the ones we invited." Charlotte rolled her eyes as sparse chuckles and giggles erupted from everyone. "Seriously, starting this new part of our lives together, we couldn't have asked for a more amazing group of people to have by our sides. Now, eat, drink and be happy. -Oh and we have to get turnt and give my boo a proper send off. London won't know what hit 'em." She finished with a wink at me.

After seemingly ignoring all of Dani's speech beforehand, Christian's head shot up to her, his whole face contorting into confusion then disbelief as he looked from Danielle to me. I smiled to Dani feeling my cheeks burn up from his stare.

"Thank you. Please excuse me everybody." I got up making my way to the bathroom, I just needed a second to cool down and remind myself that I didn't need to feel nervous; I owed him nothing, least of all an explanation. I left the restroom ready to have dessert, share some jokes and go the hell home. It's like he knew I didn't want to be around him, so in typical 'ex' fashion as soon as I open the door to the narrow corridor who do I see leaning against the wall? All this money, and these people couldn't make wider hallways?!

He pushed off of the bricked surface inching closer to me. "Why London?"

I could smell the alcohol on his breath mixed with a strong aroma of cigars. "Work", was my curt reply. Noticing my efforts to squeeze past him, he stretched his arm out blocking my path. Not saying anything, he continued cramping the passage even more by pressing himself against me. "Okay, I'm just gonna head back to the table." Having no luck pushing against his arm trying to break the barrier, I grew annoyed. "Christian, please move out of the way."

"I heard about the new boyfriend. Is he good? Does he take care of you?" He lowered his head to mine asking the questions I knew weren't as innocent as the words made them seem.

Robbing me of a retort, he grabbed my chin forcing a kiss, using my shock to shove his tongue past my lips. Beyond the bitter tang of scotch and cigars, it still tasted like him... but we weren't us so he didn't get to do this. Just as I pushed him away we heard the deafening nasal shriek.

"Christian!"

I looked to Charlotte and back to Chris before leaving the couple to themselves and going back to the table.

The night was winding down and I was beyond ready to go. Thankfully the "new boyfriend" who is not that new, was close by. Sending him a text, he replied telling me he's on his way to pick me up.

"So, A, why didn't you bring the boy tonight? He too scared to meet the family or are you not interested enough to introduce him?" He spoke with a cocky smirk that grated at my calmness.

"No, he's just one of those people who understands what a family dinner is. Plus, he's already met everyone here, with the exception of you two." I said pointing between him and Charlotte.

He looked to his grandparents and brothers with a cloud of betrayal masking his features. "What the fuck?!" He asked peering at the men.

"Christian!" Vincenzo and Winnie cautioned at the same time. His glare tightened on his grandfather, as though he wanted to fight the older man.

"You've had a little too much to drink. Let's go to the kitchen and get you some coffee."

"I'm good Vin. In fact.." He looked to the waiter and tapped the rim of his glass, gesturing for a refill. Gramps let the disrespect roll off of him, even rubbing Winnie's shoulder to deter the enraged woman from lashing out at their grandson.

"For your information, please remember I'm more family than you!" The blonde bimbo piped up, causing most of the table to roll their eyes. "Don't want to become your mother but you're acting worse, at least she didn't become a home-wrecker just to get a man." She scoffed, taking a sip of her wine.

He told her? He told her. How much did he tell her? You know what, it doesn't even matter. I didn't say anything, even veered away from his apologetically widened eyes. I heard the shuffle as Danielle stood kicking off her heels and noted how Grams tightened her grip on the fork in her hand.

"Chris, it'd be best if you take your parasite and leave now." Demetri warned through gritted teeth.

"That's okay, I think I'll call it a night. I have an early flight anyway."

Everyone began talking over one another, voicing their disapproval of my exit, while he kept quiet with his head dropped and his tramp sunk into her chair. I rose to my feet, fighting to keep the tears down when the uproar dampened long enough for Vincenzo to speak.

"Please just stay another hour. There's so much to say before you leave."

"I really should be going. I still have some last minute packing to do, but I'll be over in the morning before my flight, so you'll have plenty of time to give me the 'stranger danger' talk."

I walked around the table giving hugs and kisses to everyone before reaching him and his bitch, by then I just walked right past them to the front of the restaurant. Pulling on my jacket I take a step outside before I'm stopped by a strong grip around my arm.

"I'm sorry. I didn't know she was going to bring any of that up. I'll handle it. I promise."

"Why did she even know Christian?" I shook my head at the damaged look in his eyes. His appearance in the last year didn't skip my attention. The long unkempt hair, the scruffy beard and his leaner physique, which while still well built, was definitely not a form he'd worked on having. "Forget it, what's done is done. You don't have to handle anything, your promises don't mean shit to me anymore."

Just in time to end this chat, the car pulled up and I have never felt so thankful for someone's presence. Dressed stylishly in a 3-piece suit, he hopped out of the sports car, greeting me with a hug and kiss, pulling me from Christian's hold.

"What are you-" he looked from KC to me and back to KC, shock evident on his face like he knew him. "This is who you're dating?" His face paled as he scanned the muscular man who matched him in height, clutching me to his side.

"Goodnight Christian, you should get back inside to your wife." With that, KC opened the car door, helping me in, before making his way to the drivers' side and taking off.

Seeing him every once in a while at these family gatherings made it harder for me to deny the feelings rushing back. Especially having made an effort to avoid him after the incident at his wedding.

Looking over to KC, I played with the hair on the nape of his neck while he smiled, stroking my thigh with a free hand. Christian made his choice marrying Charlotte, and I was happy with the man right next to me.

Or at least I'm desperately trying to be.

***

Christian

Sitting in the car with Roberto at the wheel, Charlotte was still whining about my drunken kiss with Alesha, a kiss that my brain couldn't help but play on a loop. She smelt different, the scent of coconuts were gone and replaced with mangoes; it's like she tried erasing everything I loved. Still, it didn't stop me wanting to run my tongue all over her body. I was used to hearing about the changes in her life from my brothers, Grams or Richard, so seeing her in person after all this time made my subconscious flip through each memory of us, focusing on one in particular.

~

Alesha was already at my place waiting for me, and after not seeing her all day, I'm excited to get back home to my girl. Last we talked, she sounded awful proud about some surprise she'd gotten me, and considering I've been too busy to eat anything, I'm hoping the cooking lessons she asked Grams for, ties in somehow. Honestly though, at this point just seeing her face would be enough to make up for all the shit-storms I've been dealing with.

Pulling up to the house, my eyes are glued to the phone that kept pinging with all types of news alerts and texts from my family's publicist, Vanessa, about the "new girl on my arm". Sending a thanks to Roberto, I make my way up to the house, deciding to call her and shut everything down before it gets any further.

"Mr DeLuca, uh.. you didn't have to call, I know you're a busy man. I just wanted you to know your options going forward now we're dealing with the press and news outlets." She rushed out in one quick, shaky breath.

I rarely spoke to people outside of my family or businesses, so I understood why Vanessa sounded thrown-off by my call. When it came to dealing with publicists or anyone else, I usually let my grandparents take up the stress of trivial topics and questions.

"I decide my options, I'm not letting them pigeonhole me. They don't need to know anything about her. They're lucky I let them into my life as much as I already do."

"I understand, but I can't just tell reporters to stop.. reporting." The hesitation and confusion was evident in her voice.

"I'm not asking you to. I'm telling you to do your job and make sure they don't mention her." My irritation with the subject was already wearing thin.

"Sir, there are certain social responsibilities that come with you being a public figure-"

"Exactly, I'm the public figure, she is nobody's business but mine. They will tear her apart if given the opportunity, and that's not an option. Let their boards know that I give my word: if they issue anything about her, I will buy majority shares and ruin them. All of them. According to 'The Times' last print, I've got the time and money to waste, so that promise stands indefinitely until I say otherwise."

"I will try my best, Mr DeLuca."

"Vanessa, I hear Phoebe Harper is your biggest competitor."

"Yes sir, she is." Her tone seemed bewildered by my statement, maybe even anxious.

"Don't let me have to hire her instead." I hung up the phone, already having gotten my message across.

"You shouldn't be so mean to Vanessa, you'll drive the woman crazy!" I grinned at the sound of her voice shouting from whichever corner of the house she was in.

"Vanessa will be fine, her paycheck more than makes up for her bad days!" I pocketed the phone in my jeans, shrugging off my jacket to hang it up. "Why are we shouting, where are you?!"

"Bedroom!" She continued talking as I quickly made my way up to see her. "It's not about the money, it's about the principle! Lead with respect not fear!"

"People take advantage of respect! ..Fear is clear." I finished, walking into the room to see her standing by the ottoman in nothing but thinly laced lingerie.

The lights were off and candles were lit all around us, allowing the flickering lights to ricochet off of every angle of her body. I couldn't do much except stare in awe. Her deep brown skin was a shade of gold in the candlelight and her glowing eyes held so much want and lust staring back at me, while she bit her bottom lip hiding a seductive grin.

"What do you think?" She asked doing a spin which showed me every curve I was missing from where I stood.

"Are you fucking kidding me?" My heart was sitting on my throat. I could feel all the blood rushing to my lower half; the tip felt so sensitive as it hardened, rubbing against the fabric of my jeans. I stroked the swelling causing Alesha's eyes to travel down and pause on what she was doing to me.

"So you like it then." Her grin widened as she took her time closing the distance between us. I tried taking deep breaths to calm the rapid beats my dick was throbbing at; aching to be inside her.

"Why are you teasing me?" I barely managed to choke out.

She laughed pulling off my shirt, in turn making me smile. Once I was stood in front of her half-naked, her arms wrapped around me, settling on my waist. "I'm not teasing you, you can have anything you want; it's all yours." She looked up into my eyes puckering her temptingly plump lips, enticing me to lean in for a kiss.

I drew back, a little confused at the flavour on her tongue, "Cinnamon?"

"I had Cinnabon." She looked at me sarcastically with disbelief that I was ruining the moment, but all I could think was that she got Cinnabon and didn't get me anyth- "I left you some downstairs." Rolling her eyes she left another peck on my lips, and before I could even assess what was happening, my pants were unbuttoned and she was knelt in front of me.

"What are you doing?" I asked entranced but still taken aback by everything happening.

My member sprung free, making my teeth grit at the cool breeze flowing around it as she pulled my shoes, pants and boxers off each leg. My chest constricted at the sight of her full lips so close to the swollen crown of my dick.

She tried circling her fist around the entirety of my hardness, but had to settle on using both hands to massage up and down my shaft.

"I want to taste you." The simple response had my heart pounding.

Sticking her tongue out, I hissed at the sensitive touch of it flicking against the tip of my cock, making my stomach flip.

She continued with a soft but firm grasp, stroking her hands in a rotating motion along the length of me while using her tongue to lick and devour all of what could fit in her mouth. Watching the whole scene had me staring at my angel in wonder, but feeling the sensational movements had my eyes rolling back in my head.

I could feel myself hitting the back of her throat as she tried to swallow more; hearing her moans, slurps and rasps eager to taste me, only sent wild pulses to my dick, fuelling the unbearably desperate strain for her touch. She pumped faster and harder, squeezing me tighter, twisting me in her palms, her brown eyes glancing up at my face gauging the effects of her actions. Reaching back with one hand, while sucking me in and tugging at the rock-hard shaft in her sweet mouth, she started playing with my balls; even dragging her tongue along my length and toying with them between her lips at one point.

Everything she was doing had me speechless and made my heart beat faster, no-one had ever handled me like she was right now, she was flawless. Perfect.

I tried controlling my breaths, but just looking down at my woman's perfect lips drinking in my swollen cock, it didn't take too long before I was on the edge of exploding.

"Cazzo, sei cosÃ¬ bello. B-baby, I'm gonna cum."Â I stumbled out the warning expecting her to pull away. Instead, I was met with a tightened grip as she sped up, massaging the swollen boner and sucking harder.(Shit, you're so beautiful.)

Fuuck! I always feel so good inside her. It felt incredible seeing her crave me like this, this ineffable woman so ardent to please me. Breathless, I couldn't, and didn't want to, stop the warm cum that shot straight into her mouth. I already felt myself getting excited again just watching her swallow all of me.

I closed my eyes trying to shake away the black spots spinning in my head. Standing to her feet, she drew me closer trailing kisses along my collar and up my neck, then reality set in and I pulled away from her suddenly getting angry at a thought.

"You've never given me head, so where the fuck did you learn all of that?" The rush in my body died down at the expectation of an answer that was gonna have me spiralling.

"You jealous?" She was taunting me like she normally did, but there was not a fucking thing funny about it. I didn't answer, still glaring at her. Locking her darkened brown eyes onto mine, she let out an exasperated huff. "I watched some.. videos, to surprise you." She looked away, slightly embarrassed by the confession, making me regret my shitty reaction. Turning away from me, she headed for the bathroom. I grabbed her waist pulling her back and pressing my already exposed erection against her thong-clad ass; leaning to her ear.

"If I think you're doing that for anybody else I'm not just gonna be jealous, I will fuck some shit up." I ran my tongue up her neck to her earlobe, "and don't ever be embarrassed learning shit like that, as long as I'm the only one you're trying it on." I nipped at her ear feeling her cheek heat up under my nose. "You truly have no idea what I'll do for you, over you... to you."

A sexy grin was etched on her face as she turned to capture my lips, leading me backwards until I was slumped in a chair with nowhere to go. I loved seeing her take charge, pushing through her shyness to take exactly what she wanted from me.

She straddled my lap, pulling her panties to the side; I could feel her warm wet core as she rubbed me along her slick lips. Hoisting up for a second, she slowly eased her taut slit onto my dick, giving me the relief I'd been longing for all day. I observed in amazement as her eyes closed and head tilted back.

Biting on her bottom lip she started grinding on me choosing the pace and tempo. Pulling her bra down, I freed her breasts, allowing them spill over the purple lingerie. Having her hips roll against me, had me leaving tensed grips and caresses along her waist, up her stomach and across her chest.

After a bout of marvelling at her moans as she rode me, I steadied the shudder in my stomach when her rhythm stilled while her pussy clenched my greedy cock through an orgasm.

She was instantly back at it with the same momentum, trying to brace for all of me. Leaning forward, burying her face in the crook of my neck, she gently bit into my skin picking up speed. "You make me feel so good. The way.. you fill me up.. makes me wanna scream." She gasped through her raspy tone.

I was done holding back; she was too rousing and there was no pacifying my thirst for her. Slipping my hands from her thighs, she moaned louder as I grabbed her ample ass, groping and kneading the heavenly skin. Her nails dug into my biceps and her moans turned to screams as I slammed her down on me, feeling my cock hammer against her cervix; forcing her to take everything.

"Oh.. God!" Shutting her eyes tightly, her thighs hugged mine firmly, while those perfect tits with nipples hardened like smooth pebbles grazed my chest.

"You like that? You want me to make you scream?" With jaded eyes staring back at me, she nodded out of breath, her chest heavily rising and falling on mine. "You've gotta say it for me baby. You want me to make you feel good?" My tone came out as rough as my actions.

She locked our lips in a fiery kiss, playfully wrapping her tongue around mine, before pulling away with glazed eyes and a pinch at my bottom lip. "Please fuck me."

I kept pushing her down on me until she rode through another orgasm, got used to the pressure and started bouncing on my dick herself. Whatever I've done to get this woman would never have been enough to have earned her. She looked so sexy on top of me, taking everything I could give her in this moment.

She stopped, lifting off of me and I immediately missed the contact. Rising from the couch, she turned around only to settle right back on my stiffened cock. She shivered lightly as I ran my fingers down her back; delicate whimpers escaping her as her ass clapped against my lap. With my hands grasping her hips, my breath hitched when she started twirling her waist with only the tip of my dick still between her wet folds before plunging her pussy back down on me, both of our stomachs tensing at the motion. She laid her head back on my shoulder, keeping the same vivacity in her hips while I snaked my arm around her body, massaging her breasts, before reaching lower and giving her clit the attention her body was begging for.

Between the sounds of our skin smacking against one another, our deep groans and guttural moans, my high was about to peak. I rubbed at her clit until she was clawing at my hand from the sensation, provoking me to keep going. I wanted to feel her fall apart on me; and within the next few strokes, she did. Her whole body shook, limbs seizing in position; her cunt, which was engulfing my entire being, clamped around my swollen dick, draining me completely.

"I can't get enough of you." My breathing was heavy and laboured, as I brought her face to mine pressing our lips together.

"Happy Birthday." Her wheezy sentiment made us both break out in an exhausted laughter.

"Best one yet. I love you." Gazing at how radiant she looked right now, she pecked my lips again, her back deflating on my chest and her head cuddled into the crease of my neck.

"I love you too."

Her presence clouded each of my senses and I bathed in the euphoria. This is exactly how I wanted it to be for the rest of my life.

~

Even now after so long, that's still how I feel. The memory was like a tonic instantly calming every inch of me. That's all I've had to live with for the past year, memories of her. As much as I tried to, I couldn't forget her, but that's probably just because I don't actually want to. I missed her, everything about her.

Turning to Charlotte, I clasped my fist around her throat looking into those moss-green eyes.

"How the fuck did you know about Esther?"

JJ x

Epilogue - Friends Or Enemies

{ 1 Year Ago}

Christian

"I don't need your house or your money." The tears slipping from those deep brown irises made the look on her face even more heart wrenching. She turned away from me and headed for the bathroom, leaving me to stifle in the guilt. I had to get out. Picking up my bag, I left before the voice in my head telling me to stay got any louder.

Walking out of the house and stepping into the town-car, I try to remind myself of how better off she'd be without me. Roberto pulled away from the mansion and immediately my chest constricted at the idea of leaving her like that, but if I went back there's no doubt in my mind that she would convince me not to go; her cries, her words, her body, her touches, her kisses, those beautiful eyes. Fuck!

This is what's best for her, she'll find someone better and I'll... What the fuck am I gonna do?

My phone rang bringing my mental spiral to a halt. I sent the unknown number straight to voicemail not wanting to talk to anyone right now. Without a pause, the ringtone bled into my ears again, and again I hung up, frustrated that the caller didn't get the first fucking hint.

My mind travelled back to her sweet face and the thought of how much she'll probably hate me after this all settles down. She's gonna hate me. The woman that truly means everything to me, will hate me.

I can't shrug the feeling that this is a huge mistake. I can't do this.

I gave her my word that she's mine and I'm hers, always and I meant that. What the fuck am I doing, walking away from the best part of myself? I can't live without her. Shaking my head at how cliché this shit is, I pressed the intercom about to tell Roberto to turn around, but the phone's jingle sets off once more.

Growing annoyed with whoever was desperate enough to piss me off, I tap the green button on the screen.

"What?!"

"Christian?" The soft feminine voice rang out, there was something familiar about the accented voice that I couldn't quite place.

"Who is this?" I could hear the deep shaky breaths coming from the other end as the faceless caller attempted to steady herself. I don't have time for this. "Who the hell is this?" My impatience seeped through.

"Christian, it's me." It only took a second for the voice to finally click. My heart stilled as the same soft tones that told me stories and lulled me to sleep as a child were flowing through the speaker of my phone. A voice I had buried in the deepest, sweetest parts of my memories, was piercing through the walls I built years ago; knocking through the barrier faster than Alesha ever had. "Christian, can you hear me?"

My words failed to muster as all the questions and thoughts flurried around my head, only to pull one word from the cluster: "..Mom?"

***{Present Day}

"Sweetheart, where are you right now?" Charlotte asked as she looked up at me, resting her chin on my shoulder and winding her arm around mine.

"She's right Chris, you seem a little out of it tonight. Are you okay?" Richard asked from across the table noticing that my mind had wandered away from here.

"I'm good, just work still on my mind." I lied taking a swig from the glass in front of me.

"You shouldn't be thinking about work when you're with family schmoopy." Her words and that infuriating name made me send her a glare that forced her to ease off of me and lean back into her chair.

Getting married to Charlotte caused a split between us and my family, she wasn't mixing into the group as effortlessly as she had always assumed she would. She didn't get our jokes and her taste was a lot more.. decadent. They were baffled as to how a grown woman could behave so entitled and spoilt, it didn't make it any easier for her with their constant comparisons to Alesha. She didn't want to be around them and they definitely didn't want her around. I can't say I care about her discomfort though, this arrangement had its purpose, just not one I expected to drag on for so long.

"Maybe we should call it a night." Lucas suggested, probably having had his fill of faking niceties and listening to Charlotte's mindless chatter. I don't blame him. "We'll go freshen up before we get going." He gave me a knowing look before taking Charlotte's hand and leading her back to where the restaurant bathrooms were.

I pulled my attention back to Richard. "Why didn't you tell me she was going to London?"

"It's only for a few months she'll be fine. Demetri's tagging along for a month or two, he sold it to your grandparents as 'work experience' so I gave him the go-ahead to shadow the Creative Director of my London branch." I couldn't help but smile at the thought of my baby brother doing nothing but hitting on models the entire time. "Dani and Raf are spending a week of their honeymoon there too," he took a breath and looked away before continuing, "KC decided to go with her."

My fists balled at the mention of him. I wasn't sure what game KC was playing but I'll put an end to it. Last I saw him, he was beating Vasiliev to death because I gave the order, now he's strutting around with my girl on his arm?! ... Seeing him with her the other night, putting his lips on hers, touching her- I wanted to kill him, I still do and it will be that simple once all my enemies stop hiding their faces.

The last year's killed me; not knowing who was really fighting for me and everyone's true motives, had me paranoid. The one person I knew I could trust and wanted near was the one person I couldn't have close to any of this. I was at odds with myself. I couldn't be with her, but I wanted her to be happy; just not without me.

"How is she?"

"She's good. There's something missing, but that might just be me." He gave me a pursed smile coated in pity. "I think she's still trying to get over what happened with the wedding, which I should beat your ass for," he said with a raised brow, "but she's better now."

"She told you about that, huh." I felt the shame and guilt of that day easing back in.

"Just be glad it was me she told and not Dani. Speaking of Dani, has she returned any of your messages?"

"Not one. We talked a little at her wedding party the other night but that was only because she was hammered. It'll pass, we're family." I looked up to see Lucas and Charlotte already heading toward us, Richard and I stood ready to leave.

-

In the car heading home, my mind mulled over what my life is now and what it should've been. Would she even take me back after what I've put her through? She did everything she could and I shot her down at each try. She cried for me, screamed for me, fought for me, just to watch me marry Charlotte. Maybe once I've fixed everything she'll let me explain- but the things I've said to her... I fucked up.

"You're thinking about her again, aren't you?" Charlotte scoffed next to me. I zoned in to my phone scrolling through some work emails and texts. "How fucking pathetic. You have me right here and you can't help but dote on that bitch?" I wanted to wring her neck, ignoring her was taking too much effort. "You never even tried to love me like that, did you?" Her voice came out saddened and softer than usual. "We could be so happy together, Christian. You just have to give me a chance."

I looked into her eyes and wanted to feel sorry for the girl sitting in front of me, but I knew Charlotte. I knew the person she really was, all I didn't know was how mixed up in this she was. "That's not how it works. I'm staying at a hotel tonight, I have an early meeting in the city tomorrow."

The tears began pooling in her eyes as the car came to a stop in front of the mansion. She grabbed her purse and stormed out, slamming the car door shut.

I let out a sigh relieved that our night ended there. "Roberto, take me home please."

"Got it boss."

After a 30 minute drive, looking through the new photos she'd sent to Grams, who thankfully insisted on forwarding them to me, we pulled into the gated home, isolated on its own land.

Looking at the newly built house there's no doubt in my mind that she'd love it. It wasn't as big as the mansion so she wouldn't feel that alone when I'm not here, but it was fenced in with enough space and quiet for her to feel relaxed and safe.

This is where we'd grow old together.

***

"Thank you for meeting with me. I know you are a busy man, however there are a few things I have yet to get off my chest." The woman's thick Russian accent was firm and directive. Her eyes darted between Dome and the armed SUV parked outside her home. "Usually I would laugh at brutes such as yourselves taking all these precautions over a little woman like me, but knowing what my husband put you through, I understand."

I sat still, eyes trained on her pale skin and dark hair contrasted by the bright red lipstick staining her thinned lips. Her skin wearily marked by age and a deep frown sketched around her mouth. "Why did you call me here Ms Vasiliev?"

"Though I am- was a dutiful wife, I know my husband was a bastard. Between his many affairs and his conceited power from his rank in the Brotherhood, there was no hiding my hatred for him." I narrowed my eyes trying to suss out what she was getting to. "I know what he tried to do to your wife and I am forever in debt to your family for what he helped Mr Howard do." I drew in a sharp breath, gesturing for her to carry on. "I want to put this feud between our families to rest. These gangs.. it's not a world I want my children growing up in."

A clang came from the kitchen and immediately Dome drew his gun in its direction, while I held mine on Anya who jumped from her seat blocking the kitchen's doorway.

"Please! It's just my children. Что делаешь?! Я сказал вам, чтобы остаться в ваших комнатах!"(What are you doing?! I told you to stay in your rooms!)

I watched as the teen pushed in front of his mother and a much younger girl who tugged on his arm. I could see how his features favoured his father, but they both heavily resembled their mother. The sleek black hair and piercing blue eyes with the same pale white skin. The girl seemed no older than 9, but her brother looked around the same age as Demetri. I motioned to Dome to put the gun away. "Извините, мы немного на грани."(Sorry, we're a little on edge.)

"I think my mother is done talking." He looked at me with a hard stare, ignoring his mother's pleas to watch his tone. I smirked at the scene as the women failed to pull him out of view.

"It's okay." My words made Anya stop and stare at me. She held her daughter's hands stopping her movements too. "I can respect any man protecting his family." I took a step forward, with hand outstretched. "What's your name?"

He glanced from my face to my hand before clasping it in his, "Nicolai."

I shook his hand before looking to the young girl behind him. I knelt down and motioned for her to come forward. She walked to me timidly, hand still latched to her mother's. Her brother tapped her shoulder and waited for her to look to him, he moved his hands in a precise manner signing to her, immediately after his hands fell by his side, she reached up with both arms wrapping them around my neck for a hug. She let me go with a kiss on my cheek and stepped back beside her mother. "What's your name?"

As she signed something, I glanced to her brother waiting for the translation, which he gave with a smirk. "She said "Natalya, who are you?" "

I looked back at the young girl with a chuckle. "Nice to meet you Natalya, my name is Christian."

She signed again with a wide smile before her brother translated: "She says thank you for telling our dad to go away."

"That's what you told her?" I peered at him charily.

"Yes. My father deserved whatever happened to him. He was a prick, a coward and a drunk. The Bratva made a mistake choosing him, so did my mother." The older woman slapped his arm, mumbling something under her breath. He looked me over, presumably judging if he could trust me or not. "I do too." He stated abruptly.

"You do what?"

"I respect any man protecting his family. My father's cowardice and stupidity robbed us. My mother was supposed to be happy and well taken care of for the rest of her life and my sister should be going to the best schools, even though she wants to be an artist when she grows up." He scoffed with a faint smile.

"What about you?"

"The Bratva was always my future. I'll just have to join sooner than expected."

"What would you rather be doing?"

"Anything else." He blurted out, making me laugh. His mother hit him again, knowing how dangerous it was to disrespect the Bratva especially to one of its former leaders. "I'd most likely be going to school for aeronautical engineering... or some shit like that." He shrugged away the thought.

"Следите за своим ртом." Anya snapped, warning him.